THE PELICAN SHAKESPEARE
GENERAL EDITORS

STEPHEN ORGEL
A. R. BRAUNMULLER

The Life and Death of King John

Ann Barry (Mrs. Spranger Barry) as Constance in *King John*
at Drury Lane. She first acted the part in 1774, and it became
one of her great roles. She is shown at the moment of her exit
at the end of III.4, bewailing the death of her son.
From Bell's Shakespeare, 1776.

William Shakespeare

———

The Life and Death of
King John

EDITED BY CLAIRE McEACHERN

PENGUIN BOOKS

PENGUIN BOOKS

Published by the Penguin Group

Penguin Group (USA) Inc., 375 Hudson Street, New York, New York 10014, U.S.A.

Penguin Group (Canada), 90 Eglinton Avenue East, Suite 700, Toronto,
Ontario, Canada M4P 2Y3 (a division of Pearson Penguin Canada Inc.)

Penguin Books Ltd, 80 Strand, London WC2R 0RL, England

Penguin Ireland, 25 St Stephen's Green, Dublin 2, Ireland (a division of Penguin Books Ltd)

Penguin Group (Australia), 250 Camberwell Road, Camberwell,
Victoria 3124, Australia (a division of Pearson Australia Group Pty Ltd)

Penguin Books India Pvt Ltd, 11 Community Centre, Panchsheel Park, New Delhi – 110 017, India

Penguin Group (NZ), cnr Airborne and Rosedale Roads,
Albany, Auckland 1310, New Zealand (a division of Pearson New Zealand Ltd)

Penguin Books (South Africa) (Pty) Ltd, 24 Sturdee Avenue,
Rosebank, Johannesburg 2196, South Africa

Penguin Books Ltd, Registered Offices: 80 Strand, London WC2R 0RL, England

The Life and Death of King John edited by Irving Ribner published in
the United States of America in Penguin Books 1962
Revised edition published 1979
This new edition edited by Claire McEachern published 2000

3   5   7   9   10   8   6   4

Copyright © Penguin Books Inc., 1962, 1979
Copyright © Penguin Putnam Inc., 2000
All rights reserved

ISBN 0 14 07.1459 6
(CIP data available)

Printed in the United States of America
Set in Adobe Garamond
Designed by Virginia Norey

Contents

Publisher's Note

IT IS ALMOST half a century since the first volumes of the
Pelican Shakespeare appeared under the general editorship
of Alfred Harbage. The fact that a new edition, rather
than simply a revision, has been undertaken reflects the
profound changes textual and critical studies of Shakespeare have undergone in the past twenty years. For the
new Pelican series, the texts of the plays and poems have
been thoroughly revised in accordance with recent scholarship, and in some cases have been entirely reedited. New
introductions and notes have been provided in all the volumes. But the new Shakespeare is also designed as a suc-
cessor to the original series; the previous editions have
been taken into account, and the advice of the previous
editors has been solicited where it was feasible to do so.

Certain textual features of the new Pelican Shakespeare
should be particularly noted. All lines are numbered that
contain a word, phrase, or allusion explained in the
glossarial notes. In addition, for convenience, every tenth
line is also numbered, in italics when no annotation is indicated. The intrusive and often inaccurate place headings
inserted by early editors are omitted (as is becoming standard practice), but for the convenience of those who miss
them, an indication of locale now appears as the first item
in the annotation of each scene.

In the interest of both elegance and utility, each speech
prefix is set in a separate line when the speaker's lines are
in verse, except when those words form the second half of
a verse line. Thus the verse form of the speech is kept vi-
sually intact. What is printed as verse and what is printed
as prose has, in general, the authority of the original texts.
Departures from the original texts in this regard have only
the authority of editorial tradition and the judgment of
the Pelican editors; and, in a few instances, are admittedly
arbitrary.

The Theatrical World

Economic realities determined the theatrical world in which Shakespeare's plays were written, performed, and received. For centuries in England, the primary theatrical tradition was nonprofessional. Craft guilds (or "mysteries") provided religious drama – mystery plays – as part of the celebration of religious and civic festivals, and schools and universities staged classical and neoclassical drama in both Latin and English as part of their curricula. In these forms, drama was established and socially acceptable. Professional theater, in contrast, existed on the margins of society. The acting companies were itinerant; playhouses could be any available space – the great halls of the aristocracy, town squares, civic halls, inn yards, fair booths, or open fields – and income was sporadic, dependent on the passing of the hat or on the bounty of local patrons. The actors, moreover, were considered little better than vagabonds, constantly in danger of arrest or expulsion.

In the late 1560s and 1570s, however, English professional theater began to gain respectability. Wealthy aristocrats fond of drama – the Lord Admiral, for example, or the Lord Chamberlain – took acting companies under their protection so that the players technically became members of their households and were no longer subject to arrest as homeless or masterless men. Permanent theaters were first built at this time as well, allowing the companies to control and charge for entry to their performances.

Shakespeare's livelihood, and the stunning artistic explosion in which he participated, depended on pragmatic and architectural effort. Professional theater requires ways to restrict access to its offerings; if it does not, and admission fees cannot be charged, the actors do not get paid, the costumes go to a pawnbroker, and there is no such thing as a professional, ongoing theatrical tradition. The answer to that economic need arrived in the late 1560s and 1570s with the creation of the so-called public or amphitheater playhouse. Recent discoveries indicate that the precursor of the Globe playhouse in London (where Shakespeare's mature plays were presented) and the Rose theater (which presented Christopher Marlowe's plays and some of Shakespeare's earliest ones) was the Red Lion theater of 1567. Archaeological studies of the foundations of the Rose and Globe theaters have revealed that the open-air theater of the 1590s and later was probably a polygonal building with fourteen to twenty or twenty-four sides, multistoried, from 75 to 100 feet in diameter, with a raised, partly covered "thrust" stage that projected into a group of standing patrons, or "groundlings," and a covered gallery, seating up to 2,500 or more (very crowded) spectators.

These theaters might have been about half full on any given day, though the audiences were larger on holidays or when a play was advertised, as old and new were, through printed playbills posted around London. The metropolitan area's late-Tudor, early-Stuart population (circa 1590-1620) has been estimated at about 150,000 to 250,000. It has been supposed that in the mid-1590s there were about 15,000 spectators per week at the public theaters; thus, as many as 10 percent of the local population went to the theater regularly. Consequently, the theaters' repertories – the plays available for this experienced and frequent audience – had to change often: in the month between September 15 and October 15, 1595, for instance, the Lord Admiral's Men performed twenty-eight times in eighteen different plays.

Since natural light illuminated the amphitheaters' stages, performances began between noon and two o'clock and ran without a break for two or three hours. They often concluded with a jig, a fencing display, or some other nondramatic exhibition. Weather conditions determined the season for the amphitheaters: plays were performed every day (including Sundays, sometimes, to clerical dismay) except during Lent – the forty days before Easter – or periods of plague, or sometimes during the summer months when law courts were not in session and the most affluent members of the audience were not in London.

To a modern theatergoer, an amphitheater stage like that of the Rose or Globe would appear an unfamiliar mixture of plainness and elaborate decoration. Much of the structure was carved or painted, sometimes to imitate marble; elsewhere, as under the canopy projecting over the stage, to represent the stars and the zodiac. Appropriate painted canvas pictures (of Jerusalem, for example, if the play was set in that city) were apparently hung on the wall behind the acting area, and tragedies were accompanied by black hangings, presumably something like crepe festoons or bunting. Although these theaters did not employ what we would call scenery, early modern spectators saw numerous large props, such as the "bar" at which a prisoner stood during a trial, the "mossy bank" where lovers reclined, an arbor for amorous conversation, a chariot, gallows, tables, trees, beds, thrones, writing desks, and so forth. Audiences might learn a scene's location from a sign (reading "Athens," for example) carried across the stage (as in Bertolt Brecht's twentieth-century productions). Equally captivating (and equally irritating to the theater's enemies) were the rich costumes and personal props the actors used: the most valuable items in the surviving theatrical inventories are the swords, gowns, robes, crowns, and other items worn or carried by the performers.

Magic appealed to Shakespeare's audiences as much as it does to us today, and the theater exploited many deceptive and spectacular devices. A winch in the loft above the stage, called "the heavens," could lower and raise actors playing gods, goddesses, and other supernatural figures to and from the main acting area, just as one or more trapdoors permitted entrances and exits to and from the area, called "hell," beneath the stage. Actors wore elementary makeup such as wigs, false beards, and face paint, and they employed pig's bladders filled with animal blood to make wounds seem more real. They had rudimentary but effective ways of pretending to behead or hang a person. Supernumeraries (stagehands or actors not needed in a particular scene) could make thunder sounds (by shaking a metal sheet or rolling an iron ball down a chute) and show lightning (by blowing inflammable resin through tubes into a flame). Elaborate fireworks enhanced the effects of dragons flying through the air or imitated such celestial phenomena as comets, shooting stars, and multiple suns. Horses' hoofbeats, bells (located perhaps in the tower above the stage), trumpets and drums, clocks, cannon shots and gunshots, and the like were common sound effects. And the music of viols, cornets, oboes, and recorders was a regular feature of theatrical performances.

For two relatively brief spans, from the late 1570s to 1590 and from 1599 to 1614, the amphitheaters competed with the so-called private, or indoor, theaters, which originated as, or later represented themselves as, educational institutions training boys as singers for church services and court performances. These indoor theaters had two features that were distinct from the amphitheaters': their personnel and their playing spaces. The amphitheaters' adult companies included both adult men, who played the male roles, and boys, who played the female roles; the private, or indoor, theater companies, on the other hand, were entirely composed of boys aged about 8 to 16, who were, or could pretend to be, candidates for singers in a church or a royal boys' choir. (Until 1660, professional theatrical companies included no women.) The playing space would appear much more familiar to modern audiences than the long-vanished amphitheaters; the later indoor theaters were, in fact, the ancestors of the typical modern theater. They were enclosed spaces, usually rectangular, with the stage filling one end of the rectangle and the audience arrayed in seats or benches across (and sometimes lining) the building's longer axis. These spaces staged plays less frequently than the public theaters (perhaps only once a week) and held far fewer spectators than the amphitheaters: about 200 to 600, as opposed to 2,500 or more. Fewer patrons mean a smaller gross income, unless each pays more. Not surprisingly, then, private theaters charged higher prices than the amphitheaters, probably sixpence, as opposed to a penny for the cheapest entry.

Protected from the weather, the indoor theaters presented plays later in the day than the amphitheaters, and used artificial illumination – candles in sconces or candelabra. But candles melt, and need replacing, snuffing, and trimming, and these practical requirements may have been part of the reason the indoor theaters introduced breaks in the performance, the intermission so dear to the heart of theatergoers and to the pocketbooks of theater concessionaires ever since. Whether motivated by the need to tend to the candles or by the entrepreneurs' wishing to sell oranges and liquor, or both, the indoor theaters eventually established the modern convention of the non-continuous performance. In the early modern "private" theater, musical performances apparently filled the intermissions, which in Stuart theater jargon seem to have been called "acts."

At the end of the first decade of the seventeenth century, the distinction between public amphitheaters and private indoor companies ceased. For various cultural, political, and economic reasons, individual companies gained control of both the public, open-air theaters and the indoor ones, and companies mixing adult men and boys took over the formerly "private" theaters. Despite the death of the boys' companies and of their highly innovative theaters (for which such luminous playwrights as Ben Jonson, George Chapman, and John Marston wrote), their playing spaces and conventions had an immense impact on subsequent plays: not merely for the intervals (which stressed the artistic and architectonic importance of "acts"), but also because they introduced political and social satire as a popular dramatic ingredient, even in tragedy, and a wider range of actorly effects, encouraged by their more intimate playing spaces.

Even the briefest sketch of the Shakespearean theatrical world would be incomplete without some comment on the social and cultural dimensions of theaters and playing in the period. In an intensely hierarchical and status-conscious society, professional actors and their ventures had hardly any respectability; as we have indicated, to protect themselves against laws designed to curb vagabondage and the increase of masterless men, actors resorted to the near-fiction that they were the servants of noble masters, and wore their distinctive livery. Hence the company for which Shakespeare wrote in the 1590s called itself the Lord Chamberlain's Men and pretended that the public, money-getting performances were in fact rehearsals for private performances before that high court official. From 1598, the Privy Council had licensed theatrical companies, and after 1603, with the accession of King James I, the companies gained explicit royal protection, just as the Queen's Men had for a time under Queen Elizabeth. The Chamberlain's Men became the King's Men, and the other companies were patronized by the other members of the royal family.

These designations were legal fictions that half-concealed an important economic and social development, the evolution away from the theater's organization on the model of the guild, a self-regulating confraternity of individual artisans, into a proto-capitalist organization. Shakespeare's company became a joint-stock company, where persons who supplied capital and, in some cases, such as Shakespeare's, capital and talent, employed themselves and others in earning a return on that capital. This development meant that actors and theater companies were outside both the traditional guild structures, which required some form of civic or royal charter, and the feudal household organization of master-and-servant. This anomalous, maverick social and economic condition made theater companies practically unruly and potentially even dangerous; consequently, numerous official bodies – including the London metropolitan and ecclesiastical authorities as well as, occasionally, the royal court itself – tried, without much success, to control and even to disband them.

Public officials had good reason to want to close the theaters: they were attractive nuisances – they drew often riotous crowds, they were always noisy, and they could be politically offensive and socially insubordinate. Until the Civil War, however, anti-theatrical forces failed to shut down professional theater, for many reasons – limited surveillance and few police powers, tensions or outright hostilities among the agencies that sought to check or channel theatrical activity, and lack of clear policies for control. Another reason must have been the theaters' undeniable popularity. Curtailing any activity enjoyed by such a substantial percentage of the population was difficult, as various Roman emperors attempting to limit circuses had learned, and the Tudor-Stuart audience was not merely large, it was socially diverse and included women. The prevalence of public entertainment in this period has been underestimated. In fact, fairs, holidays, games, sporting events, the equivalent of modern parades, freak shows, and street exhibitions all abounded, but the theater was the most widely and frequently available entertainment to which people of every class had access. That fact helps account both for its quantity and for the fear and anger it aroused.

WILLIAM SHAKESPEARE OF
STRATFORD-UPON-AVON, GENTLEMAN

Many people have said that we know very little about William Shakespeare's life – pinheads and postcards are often mentioned as appropriately tiny surfaces on which to record the available information. More imaginatively and perhaps more correctly, Ralph Waldo Emerson wrote, "Shakespeare is the only biographer of Shakespeare. . . . So far from Shakespeare's being the least known, he is the one person in all modern history fully known to us."

In fact, we know more about Shakespeare's life than we do about almost any other English writer's of his era. His last will and testament (dated March 25, 1616) survives, as do numerous legal contracts and court documents involving Shakespeare as principal or witness, and parish records in Stratford and London. Shakespeare appears quite often in official records of King James's royal court, and of course Shakespeare's name appears on numerous title pages and in the written and recorded words of his literary contemporaries Robert Greene, Henry Chettle, Francis Meres, John Davies of Hereford, Ben Jonson, and many others. Indeed, if we make due allowance for the bloating of modern, run-of-the-mill bureaucratic records, more information has survived over the past four hundred years about William Shakespeare of Stratford-upon-Avon, Warwickshire, than is likely to survive in the next four hundred years about any reader of these words.

What we do not have are entire categories of information – Shakespeare's private letters or diaries, drafts and revisions of poems and plays, critical prefaces or essays, commendatory verse for other writers' works, or instructions guiding his fellow actors in their performances, for instance – that we imagine would help us understand and appreciate his surviving writings. For all we know, many such data never existed as written records. Many literary and theatrical critics, not knowing what might once have existed, more or less cheerfully accept the situation; some even make a theoretical virtue of it by claiming that such data are irrelevant to understanding and interpreting the plays and poems.

So, what do we know about William Shakespeare, the man responsible for thirty-seven or perhaps more plays, more than 150 sonnets, two lengthy narrative poems, and some shorter poems?

While many families by the name of Shakespeare (or some variant spelling) can be identified in the English Midlands as far back as the twelfth century, it seems likely that the dramatist's grandfather, Richard, moved to Snitterfield, a town not far from Stratford-upon-Avon, sometime before 1529. In Snitterfield, Richard Shakespeare leased farmland from the very wealthy Robert Arden. By 1552, Richard's son John had moved to a large house on Henley Street in Stratford-upon-Avon, the house that stands today as "The Birthplace." In Stratford, John Shakespeare traded as a glover, dealt in wool, and lent money at interest; he also served in a variety of civic posts, including "High Bailiff," the municipality's equivalent of mayor. In 1557, he married Robert Arden's youngest daughter, Mary. Mary and John had four sons – William was the oldest – and four daughters, of whom only Joan outlived her most celebrated sibling. William was baptized (an event entered in the Stratford parish church records) on April 26, 1564, and it has become customary, without any good factual support, to suppose he was born on April 23, which happens to be the feast day of Saint George, patron saint of England, and is also the date on which he died, in 1616. Shakespeare married Anne Hathaway in 1582, when he was eighteen and she was twenty-six; their first child was born five months later. It has been generally assumed that the marriage was enforced and subsequently unhappy, but these are only assumptions; it has been estimated, for instance, that up to one third of Elizabethan brides were pregnant when they married. Anne and William Shakespeare had three children: Susanna, who married a prominent local physician, John Hall; and the twins Hamnet, who died young in 1596, and Judith, who married Thomas Quiney – apparently a rather shady individual. The name Hamnet was unusual but not unique: he and his twin sister were named for their godparents, Shakespeare's neighbors Hamnet and Judith Sadler. Shakespeare's father died in 1601 (the year of *Hamlet*), and Mary Arden Shakespeare died in 1608 (the year of *Coriolanus*). William Shakespeare's last surviving direct descendant was his granddaughter Elizabeth Hall, who died in 1670.

Between the birth of the twins in 1585 and a clear reference to Shakespeare as a practicing London dramatist in Robert Greene's sensationalizing, satiric pamphlet, *Greene's Groatsworth of Wit* (1592), there is no record of where William Shakespeare was or what he was doing. These seven so-called lost years have been imaginatively filled by scholars and other students of Shakespeare: some think he traveled to Italy, or fought in the Low Countries, or studied law or medicine, or worked as an apprentice actor/writer, and so on to even more fanciful possibilities. Whatever the biographical facts for those "lost" years, Greene's nasty remarks in 1592 testify to professional envy and to the fact that Shakespeare already had a successful career in London. Speaking to his fellow playwrights, Greene warns both generally and specifically:

> . . . trust them [actors] not: for there is an upstart crow, beautified with our feathers, that with his tiger's heart wrapped in a player's hide supposes he is as well able to bombast out a blank verse as the best of you; and being an absolute Johannes Factotum, is in his own conceit the only Shake-scene in a country.

The passage mimics a line from *3 Henry VI* (hence the play must have been performed before Greene wrote) and seems to say that "Shake-scene" is both actor and play-wright, a jack-of-all-trades. That same year, Henry Chettle protested Greene's remarks in *Kind-Heart's Dream,* and each of the next two years saw the publication of poems – *Venus and Adonis* and *The Rape of Lucrece,* respectively – publicly ascribed to (and dedicated by) Shakespeare. Early in 1595 he was named one of the senior members of a prominent acting company, the Lord Chamberlain's Men, when they received payment for court performances during the 1594 Christmas season.

Clearly, Shakespeare had achieved both success and reputation in London. In 1596, upon Shakespeare's application, the College of Arms granted his father the now-familiar coat of arms he had taken the first steps to obtain almost twenty years before, and in 1598, John's son – now permitted to call himself "gentleman" – took a 10 percent share in the new Globe playhouse. In 1597, he bought a substantial bourgeois house, called New Place, in Stratford – the garden remains, but Shakespeare's house, several times rebuilt, was torn down in 1759 – and over the next few years Shakespeare spent large sums buying land and making other investments in the town and its environs. Though he worked in London, his family remained in Stratford, and he seems always to have considered Stratford the home he would eventually return to. Something approaching a disinterested appreciation of Shakespeare's popular and professional status appears in Francis Meres's *Palladis Tamia* (1598), a not especially imaginative and perhaps therefore persuasive record of literary reputations. Reviewing contemporary English writers, Meres lists the titles of many of Shakespeare's plays, including one not now known, *Love's Labor's Won,* and praises his "mellifluous & hony-tongued" "sugred Sonnets," which were then circulating in manuscript (they were first collected in 1609). Meres describes Shakespeare as "one of the best" English playwrights of both comedy and tragedy. In *Remains . . . Concerning Britain* (1605),

William Camden – a more authoritative source than the imitative Meres – calls Shakespeare one of the "most pregnant witts of these our times" and joins him with such writers as Chapman, Daniel, Jonson, Marston, and Spenser. During the first decades of the seventeenth century, publishers began to attribute numerous play quartos, including some non-Shakespearean ones, to Shakespeare, either by name or initials, and we may assume that they deemed Shakespeare's name and supposed authorship, true or false, commercially attractive.

For the next ten years or so, various records show Shakespeare's dual career as playwright and man of the theater in London, and as an important local figure in Stratford. In 1608-9 his acting company – designated the "King's Men" soon after King James had succeeded Queen Elizabeth in 1603 – rented, refurbished, and opened a small interior playing space, the Blackfriars theater, in London, and Shakespeare was once again listed as a substantial sharer in the group of proprietors of the playhouse. By May 11, 1612, however, he describes himself as a Stratford resident in a London lawsuit – an indication that he had withdrawn from day-to-day professional activity and returned to the town where he had always had his main financial interests. When Shakespeare bought a substantial residential building in London, the Blackfriars Gatehouse, close to the theater of the same name, on March 10, 1613, he is recorded as William Shakespeare "of Stratford upon Avon in the county of Warwick, gentleman," and he named several London residents as the building's trustees. Still, he continued to participate in theatrical activity: when the new Earl of Rutland needed an allegorical design to bear as a shield, or *impresa,* at the celebration of King James's Accession Day, March 24, 1613, the earl's accountant recorded a payment of 44 shillings to Shakespeare for the device with its motto.

For the last few years of his life, Shakespeare evidently

concentrated his activities in the town of his birth. Most of the final records concern business transactions in Stratford, ending with the notation of his death on April 23, 1616, and burial in Holy Trinity Church, Stratford-upon-Avon.

THE QUESTION OF AUTHORSHIP

The history of ascribing Shakespeare's plays (the poems do not come up so often) to someone else began, as it continues, peculiarly. The earliest published claim that someone else wrote Shakespeare's plays appeared in an 1856 article by Delia Bacon in the American journal *Putnam's Monthly* – although an Englishman, Thomas Wilmot, had shared his doubts in private (even secretive) conversations with friends near the end of the eighteenth century. Bacon's was a sad personal history that ended in madness and poverty, but the year after her article, she published, with great difficulty and the bemused assistance of Nathaniel Hawthorne (then United States Consul in Liverpool, England), her *Philosophy of the Plays of Shakspere Unfolded.* This huge, ornately written, confusing farrago is almost unreadable; sometimes its intents, to say nothing of its arguments, disappear entirely beneath near-raving, ecstatic writing. Tumbled in with much supposed "philosophy" appear the claims that Francis Bacon (from whom Delia Bacon eventually claimed descent), Walter Ralegh, and several other contemporaries of Shakespeare's had written the plays. The book had little impact except as a ridiculed curiosity.

Once proposed, however, the issue gained momentum among people whose conviction was the greater in proportion to their ignorance of sixteenth- and seventeenth-century English literature, history, and society. Another American amateur, Catherine P. Ashmead Windle, made the next influential contribution to the cause when she published *Report to the British Museum* (1882), wherein she promised to open "the Cipher of Francis Bacon," though what she mostly offers, in the words of S. Schoenbaum, is "demented allegorizing." An entire new cottage industry grew from Windle's suggestion that the texts contain hidden, cryptographically discoverable ciphers – "clues" – to their authorship; and today there are not only books devoted to the putative ciphers, but also pamphlets, journals, and newsletters.

Although Baconians have led the pack of those seeking a substitute Shakespeare, in *"Shakespeare" Identified* (1920), J. Thomas Looney became the first published "Oxfordian" when he proposed Edward de Vere, seventeenth earl of Oxford, as the secret author of Shakespeare's plays. Also for Oxford and his "authorship" there are today dedicated societies, articles, journals, and books. Less popular candidates – Queen Elizabeth and Christopher Marlowe among them – have had adherents, but the movement seems to have divided into two main contending factions, Baconian and Oxfordian. (For further details on all the candidates for "Shakespeare," see S. Schoenbaum, *Shakespeare's Lives,* 2nd ed., 1991.)

The Baconians, the Oxfordians, and supporters of other candidates have one trait in common – they are snobs. Every pro-Bacon or pro-Oxford tract sooner or later claims that the historical William Shakespeare of Stratford-upon-Avon could not have written the plays because he could not have had the training, the university education, the experience, and indeed the imagination or background their author supposedly possessed. Only a learned genius like Bacon or an aristocrat like Oxford could have written such fine plays. (As it happens, lucky male children of the middle class had access to better education than most aristocrats in Elizabethan England – and Oxford was not particularly well educated.) Shakespeare received in the Stratford grammar school a formal education that would daunt many college graduates today; and popular rival playwrights such as the very learned Ben Jonson and George Chapman, both of whom also lacked university training, achieved great artistic success, without being taken as Bacon or Oxford.

Besides snobbery, one other quality characterizes the authorship controversy: lack of evidence. A great deal of testimony from Shakespeare's time shows that Shakespeare wrote Shakespeare's plays and that his contemporaries recognized them as distinctive and distinctly superior. (Some of that contemporary evidence is collected in E. K. Chambers, *William Shakespeare: A Study of Facts and Problems,* 2 vols., 1930.) Since that testimony comes from Shakespeare's enemies and theatrical competitors as well as from his co-workers and from the Elizabethan equivalent of literary journalists, it seems unlikely that, if any one of these sources had known he was a fraud, they would have failed to record that fact.

Books About Shakespeare's Theater

Useful scholarly studies of theatrical life in Shakespeare's day include: G. E. Bentley, *The Jacobean and Caroline Stage,* 7 vols. (1941-68), and the same author's *The Professions of Dramatist and Player in Shakespeare's Time, 1590-1642* (1986); E. K. Chambers, *The Elizabethan Stage,* 4 vols. (1923); R. A. Foakes, *Illustrations of the English Stage, 1580-1642* (1985); Andrew Gurr, *The Shakespearean Stage,* 3rd ed. (1992), and the same author's *Play-going in Shakespeare's London,* 2nd ed. (1996); Edwin Nungezer, *A Dictionary of Actors* (1929); Carol Chillington Rutter, ed., *Documents of the Rose Playhouse* (1984).

Books About Shakespeare's Life

The following books provide scholarly, documented accounts of Shakespeare's life: G. E. Bentley, *Shakespeare: A Biographical Handbook* (1961); E. K. Chambers, *William Shakespeare: A Study of Facts and Problems,* 2 vols. (1930); S. Schoenbaum, *William Shakespeare: A Compact*

Documentary Life (1977); and *Shakespeare's Lives,* 2nd ed. (1991), by the same author. Many scholarly editions of Shakespeare's complete works print brief compilations of essential dates and events. References to Shakespeare's works up to 1700 are collected in C. M. Ingleby et al., *The Shakespeare Allusion-Book,* rev. ed., 2 vols. (1932).

The Texts of Shakespeare

As FAR AS WE KNOW, only one manuscript conceivably in Shakespeare's own hand may (and even this is much disputed) exist: a few pages of a play called *Sir Thomas More*, which apparently was never performed. What we do have, as later readers, performers, scholars, students, are printed texts. The earliest of these survive in two forms: quartos and folios. Quartos (from the Latin for "four") are small books, printed on sheets of paper that were then folded in fours, to make eight double-sided pages. When these were bound together, the result was a squarish, eminently portable volume that sold for the relatively small sum of sixpence (translating in modern terms to about $5.00). In folios, on the other hand, the sheets are folded only once, in half, producing large, impressive volumes taller than they are wide. This was the format for important works of philosophy, science, theology, and literature (the major precedent for a folio Shakespeare was Ben Jonson's *Works,* 1616). The decision to print the works of a popular playwright in folio is an indication of how far up on the social scale the theatrical profession had come during Shakespeare's lifetime. The Shakespeare folio was an expensive book, selling for between fifteen and eighteen shillings, depending on the binding (in modern terms, from about $150 to $180). Twenty Shakespeare plays of the thirty-seven that survive first appeared in quarto, seventeen of which appeared during Shakespeare's lifetime; the rest of the plays are found only in folio.

The First Folio was published in 1623, seven years after Shakespeare's death, and was authorized by his fellow actors, the co-owners of the King's Men. This publication was certainly a mark of the company's enormous respect for Shakespeare; but it was also a way of turning the old plays, most of which were no longer current in the playhouse, into ready money (the folio includes only Shakespeare's plays, not his sonnets or other nondramatic verse). Whatever the motives behind the publication of the folio, the texts it preserves constitute the basis for almost all later editions of the playwright's works. The texts, however, differ from those of the earlier quartos, sometimes in minor respects but often significantly – most strikingly in the two texts of *King Lear,* but also in important ways in *Hamlet, Othello,* and *Troilus and Cressida.* (The variants are recorded in the textual notes to each play in the new Pelican series.) The differences in these texts represent, in a sense, the essence of theater: the texts of plays were initially not intended for publication. They were scripts, designed for the actors to perform – the principal life of the play at this period was in performance. And it follows that in Shakespeare's theater the playwright typically had no say either in how his play was performed or in the disposition of his text – he was an employee of the company. The authoritative figures in the theatrical enterprise were the shareholders in the company, who were for the most part the major actors. They decided what plays were to be done; they hired the playwright and often gave him an outline of the play they wanted him to write. Often, too, the play was a collaboration: the company would retain a group of writers, and parcel out the scenes among them. The resulting script was then the property of the company, and the actors would revise it as they saw fit during the course of putting it on stage. The resulting text belonged to the company. The playwright had no rights in it once he had been paid. (This system survives largely intact in the movie industry, and most of the playwrights of Shakespeare's time were as anonymous as most screenwriters are today.) The script could also, of course, continue to change as the tastes of audiences and the requirements of the actors changed. Many – perhaps most – plays were revised when they were reintroduced after any substantial absence from the repertory, or when they were performed by a company different from the one that originally commissioned the play.

Shakespeare was an exceptional figure in this world because he was not only a shareholder and actor in his company, but also its leading playwright – he was literally his own boss. He had, moreover, little interest in the publication of his plays, and even those that appeared during his lifetime with the authorization of the company show no signs of any editorial concern on the part of the author. Theater was, for Shakespeare, a fluid and supremely responsive medium – the very opposite of the great classic canonical text that has embodied his works since 1623.

The very fluidity of the original texts, however, has meant that Shakespeare has always had to be edited. Here is an example of how problematic the editorial project inevitably is, a passage from the most famous speech in *Romeo and Juliet,* Juliet's balcony soliloquy beginning "O Romeo, Romeo, wherefore art thou Romeo?" Since the eighteenth century, the standard modern text has read,

> What's Montague? It is nor hand, nor foot,
> Nor arm, nor face, nor any other part
> Belonging to a man. O be some other name!
> What's in a name? That which we call a rose
> By any other name would smell as sweet.
> (II.2.40–44)

Editors have three early texts of this play to work from, two quarto texts and the folio. Here is how the First Quarto (1597) reads:

> Whats *Mountague?* It is nor hand nor foote,
> Nor arme, nor face, nor any other part.
> Whats in a name? That which we call a Rose,
> By any other name would smell as sweet:

Here is the Second Quarto (1599):

> Whats *Mountague?* it is nor hand nor foote,
> Nor arme nor face, ô be some other name
> Belonging to a man.
> Whats in a name that which we call a rose,
> By any other word would smell as sweete,

And here is the First Folio (1623):

> What's *Mountague?* it is nor hand nor foote,
> Nor arme, nor face, O be some other name
> Belonging to a man.
> What? in a names that which we call a Rose,
> By any other word would smell as sweete,

There is in fact no early text that reads as our modern text does – and this is the most famous speech in the play. Instead, we have three quite different texts, all of which are clearly some version of the same speech, but none of which seems to us a final or satisfactory version. The transcendently beautiful passage in modern editions is an editorial invention: editors have succeeded in conflating and revising the three versions into something we recognize as great poetry. Is this what Shakespeare "really" wrote? Who can say? What we can say is that Shakespeare always had performance, not a book, in mind.

Books About the Shakespeare Texts

The standard study of the printing history of the First Folio is W. W. Greg, *The Shakespeare First Folio* (1955). J. K. Walton, *The Quarto Copy for the First Folio of Shakespeare*

(1971), is a useful survey of the relation of the quartos to the folio. The second edition of Charlton Hinman's *Norton Facsimile* of the First Folio (1996), with a new introduction by Peter Blayney, is indispensable. Stanley Wells and Gary Taylor, *William Shakespeare: A Textual Companion,* keyed to the Oxford text, gives a comprehensive survey of the editorial situation for all the plays and poems.

THE GENERAL EDITORS

Introduction

THE POLITICAL WORLD of *King John* is one of precarious and sudden movement, a place where actions repeatedly outrun intentions, where the strategies of kings – when even clearly present – are repeatedly intruded upon by greater political circumstances as well as the entrepreneurial innovations of unusual political actors. Shakespeare gives us a universe where state government as an enterprise of established institutions has yet to arrive, where the certainties and sanctities of a later time have yet to emerge; this is an environment in which political process seems to be influenced equally by chaotic accident and opportunistic energies, where chance is as likely to govern the course of nations as providence is.

The Life and Death of King John is in a sense an anomaly among Shakespeare's plays about English history, the majority of which deal with the political fortunes and persons of the fifteenth century, those immediately antecedent to, and generative of, the Tudor regime of Shakespeare's England. *King John,* rather, treats materials of the late thirteenth century. It offers a king both ahead of his time and yet one whose reign is remote from some of the political commonplaces that were familiar to Shakespeare and his audience, such as a monarch with a long-established claim to the throne, a state church independent of papal control, or a national geographical polity largely bounded by the boundaries of the British isles. The play imagines an England in which later political verities appear, as it were, in utero, but it is also one in which the past does indeed seem a foreign country, and the route between the thirteenth century and the late sixteenth seems neither direct nor easily traveled.

The play opens with the troubling question of how power is transferred between generations. In the opening scene King John gives audience to the French ambassador, who delivers the news that France contests, on behalf of John's nephew Arthur, John's "borrowed majesty" and his right to the English throne (I.1.4). The two claims and countries square off against each other in a kind of political symmetry: "Here have we war for war and blood for blood, / Controlment for controlment" (I.1.19-20). Yet it soon appears that the symmetry is a stalemate, that the "right and true behalf" of Arthur must contend with the rival claim of his uncle: an Angiers citizen comments, "Both are alike, and both alike we like" (II.1.331). At the heart of the issue are the ways and means of patrilineal power. Does the throne belong to Arthur because he is the eldest son of John's elder brother Geoffrey, and so prior, despite his youth, in the dynastic birth order? Or does John's claim to his elder brother Richard's throne override his nephew's title, especially since a "strong possession" is in these matters nine tenths of the law? How does political power move through time? If majesty can be "borrowed," is it ever truly owned or bequeathed? While all parties in this world repeatedly invoke the language of rightful succession and divine sanction on behalf of lineal transfers of authority, the decorum of orderly father-to-son transmission has yet to establish itself in the play as anything other than an appealing fiction (indeed, as a legal practice, primogeniture began to be established in the common law only in the reigns of Henry II and John – a fact that Shakespeare could have read in Holinshed). As if to underscore the point that political ideals exist at some distance from actual events, the high political ceremony with which the play opens is rudely interrupted by a domestic dispute that seems to belong more to the theater of farce than of foreign policy. However, the local conflict between the brothers Faulconbridge – who is the true heir to their father's land? – reiterates the impasse troubling the highest political reaches. Kings and their subjects alike confound issues of priority and lineage.

The question of priority and descent is one that also bedevils the literary genesis and authority of *The Life and Death of King John,* and it is a question that reflects upon our understanding of the play's date and source. Shakespeare's play is one of two on this subject from the last decade of the sixteenth century. It shares its monarch, plot, and even some of its verse with another play, titled *The Troublesome Reign of King John.* Both of these plays are indebted to the second edition of the *Chronicles* of English history of Raphael Holinshed, which was published in London in 1587, and thus the two plays must postdate that year. The text of *The Troublesome Reign* was published in quarto in 1591, and again – first (erroneously) under Shakespeare's initials and then name – in 1611 and 1622; the earliest text we have of *The Life and Death of King John* is the First Folio, of 1623, although the Elizabethan literary commentator Francis Meres lists the play among Shakespeare's works as of 1598. Scholars have debated which of these plays was written or performed first, and whether either is indebted to the other, basing their analyses on style, narrative structure, and possible topical allusions. The inquiry is, as such inquiries inevitably are, vexed by notions of Shakespeare's literary superiority and originality. The question is perhaps irresolvable; the most recent judicious verdict is that of A. R. Braunmuller, who dates the composition and performance of *King John* to the years 1595-96 – the years of *Romeo and Juliet* and of *Richard II.**

The untoward sequence of the opening scene, in which royal plans and their ceremonial protocols are upstaged and intruded upon by unexpected events and persons, is one that is repeated throughout the play. In Act Two, the

---

* A. R. Braunmuller, ed., *King John* (New York: Oxford University Press, 1994), p. 15.

kings of France and England face off against each other in person, this time with armies behind them. Their language is as heavy, if not even weightier, than their artillery. Both sides claim the throne of England and the town of Angiers: King John announces his "just and lineal entrance to our own" (II.1.85); King Philip of France derives his authority "From that supernal judge that stirs good thoughts / In any breast of strong authority, / To look into the blots and stains of right" (II.1.112-14). They soon cease trying to convince each other, however, and turn to the town they would enter to arbitrate their claims. This is an extraordinary (and even risky) move for royalty – to ask of its subjects whose power they recognize. It is a gesture that perhaps indicates the difficulty of being a king in this world. Neither king's rhetoric, however impressive, is of any use before the cagey citizens of Angiers, who reply merely, "In brief, we are the King of England's subjects . . . he that proves the king, / To him will we prove loyal" (II.1.267-71). Proof of who is king, of course, is precisely the problem. Is it might? Right? Or the possession of the signs and symbols of royalty? As John asks, "Doth not the crown of England prove the king?" (II.1.273). (Ironically, John has himself crowned more than once in the play, a habit that may have been unremarkable as a medieval practice but has the effect here of protesting a bit too much – as Salisbury reproves him, "It makes the course of thoughts to fetch about, / Startles and frights consideration," IV.2.24-25.)

Small wonder is it that in this universe kings have far less freedom of action than others when it comes to political enterprise. Significantly, it is neither king nor army that resolves the impasse before the gates of Angiers, but two civilians: first Philip the Bastard, with his incendiary plot to join enemy forces against the city, and then Hubert, with his diplomatic plan to join French and English forces through the marriage of King John's niece Blanche and Lewis, the Dauphin of France. This coup has the effect of severing the bond between France and Arthur necessary to the latter's pursuit of the English throne.

The fact that the resolution and eventual reprise of this conflict comes not from the highest reaches of power but from more unexpected quarters points to the vulnerability of these kings to forces beyond their control: the weather, their relatives, or the pope. Some of these forces are smaller than kingship, and some are larger. King Philip's eventual capitulation to the threats of Rome in breaking his truce (despite the marital alliance with England) would have pointed out to Shakespeare's audience the sheer alterity of royal rule in a moment where a national church had yet to break free of papal control. Henry VIII had declared in 1533, "this realm of England is an empire," and hence subject to no foreign dominion. The independence of the monarch from the control of extranational political structures (e.g., the papacy) was a dear tenet of Elizabethan patriotism. Among medieval kings, King John was a kind of hero for English Protestantism, and authors such as John Bale, in his play *King Johan* (performed 1539?) imagined him as a touchstone of Reformation propaganda, vilifying the interference of the papacy in national affairs (interestingly, the reputation that King John enjoys in modern times, as a granter of the Magna Carta, receives no mention in Elizabethan treatments of his reign).

Shakespeare's King John bangs the same antipapal drum in this play, when he declaims, in true Elizabethan Protestant fashion, "no Italian priest / Shall tithe or toll in our dominions" (III.1.153-54) or "I alone, alone do me oppose / Against the pope, and count his friends my foes" (III.1.170-71). These are, however, boasts easier to make than to make good on in the thirteenth century, and we see John himself ultimately return to the church for sanction and support, and a means to subdue a rebellious populace incited by that very papacy to revolt: "from his holiness use all your power / To stop their marches 'fore we are "inflamed" (V.1.6-7). Alas, despite this capitulation to the power of the pope, John dies an ignominious death at the (allegedly) poisoning hand of a monk (though in this, Shakespeare gives him a somewhat flattering demise, since the historical King John reputedly succumbed only to overeating). At the end of the play, only Lewis, the Dauphin of France, still brashly voices resistance to the pope and his deputy, as the latter tries to dissuade him from a war he has set in motion: "Am I Rome's slave? What penny hath Rome borne, / What men provided, what munition sent, / To underprop this action? Is 't not I / That undergo this charge?" (V.2.97-100). This is not, however, a tenable position, at least not for very long, and even the dauphin (his supplies lost, and his allies defected) makes terms with the church in the end. Royal defiance of papal power is as yet merely rhetorical.

The powerful way in which the church operates in this world, making and suspending treaties, instigating and quelling rebellions, excommunicating and crowning kings, would have seemed to Shakespeare's audience a lurid and also salient portrait of papal dominion. Given that the pope had issued in 1570 a papal bull (or decree) excommunicating Queen Elizabeth and pardoning anyone who would resist her authority, the role of Cardinal Pandulph in this play would have seemed an especially sinister one. At the same time, the play points out the historical particularity and vulnerability of the institution of kingship, that being a king means different things in different historical moments and geopolitical configurations. It may be Philip of France who says, in some dismay, "I am perplexed, and know not what to say" (III.1.221) when confronted by the specter of Rome's displeasure. But the very plaintive dependence (however French) of kings in this play upon an external temporal sanction would have put in a precious light the tenet of Elizabethan England that held that the monarch, rather than the pope, is God's representative on earth and answerable to no one but that divinity.

However, if a truly convincing vision of royal power is present in this play only by negation, or anticipation, there is also a suggestion it was not always thus. The ghost of Richard Coeur de Lion haunts the play in the dual – and equally dubious – forms of a vigorous bastard son and the remnant of a lion skin. Neither is a particularly satisfying totem of a once-glamorous royal power. The myth of Richard Plantagenet is of a virile and potent chivalric king-errant, slayer of lions and ladies alike. But his presence can be apprehended only nostalgically, much like that of Saint George, the patron saint of English chivalry who, as the Bastard cavalierly says, "swinged the dragon, and e'er since / Sits on's horseback at mine hostess' door" (II.1.288-89). The pilgrimage from saint to tavern sign is an ignominious one. If the powerful men of this play have yet to benefit from sixteenth-century forms of political authority, they also lack the quasi-mystical and mythical power of a legendary – now moth-eaten – chivalry. King John must govern in a world where kingship has lost the power of romance and has yet to be resanctified by a politically convincing myth of divine right.

However, the weak power of kings makes space for a new kind of political actor. The play is populated by figures whose claim to legitimate authority, and even to historical veracity, may be scant, but who nonetheless impact heavily and decisively on the events in question. The actions of characters such as Hubert and the Bastard are pivotal in terms of political events; so too the presence of Arthur, Eleanor, Constance, and Blanche packs an untoward affective and political punch.

The first crisis of the play is largely moderated not by the kings of England and France, but Sir Richard Plantagenet (formerly Philip Faulconbridge) and Hubert: the former is dedicated to inciting violence, and the latter, to avoiding it. The Bastard hopes that the kings will unite their forces against the recalcitrant Angiers: "Be friends awhile and both conjointly bend / Your sharpest deeds of malice on this town" (II.1.379-80). Hubert's plan to marry John's niece Blanche to the French dauphin (and hence to transfer France's support for Arthur's claim to a promise of a more certain, less bloody access to greater territory) is, as the Bastard ruefully recognizes, "a stay, / That shakes the rotten carcase of old Death / Out of his rags!" (II.1.455-57). Unlikely gods of war and peace, the Bastard and Hubert operate in opposing fashions throughout much of the course of the action. This contrast persists even when they are united as John's two chief henchmen, as if King John were the protagonist of a morality play, and Hubert and the Bastard his opposing angels. Hubert, for instance, seeks a way to avoid killing Arthur, while the Bastard seeks to rouse King John and his troops to necessary action, as if to rouse the spirit of his lionhearted elder brother: "Be stirring as the time; be fire with fire. / Threaten the threat'ner, and outface the brow / Of bragging horror" (V.1.48-50). Together, these two figures – both Shakespeare's inventions – propel much of the action, as if to emphasize that the more remote a character is from power, the more political agility and opportunity to influence historical events he possesses.

This is an inverse proportion available even to Arthur, the unwilling child claimant to the English throne. Though his identity throughout the play is that of a reluctant political actor, even he, in his apparent weakness, is capable of autonomous enterprise. His power lies in his very powerlessness. Sheerly through his rhetorical deployment of his own plight he manages to outwit John's plan to blind him, proving that an effectively marshaled pathos is as powerful as brute force; when he attempts an escape, which ends in his effective suicide, he influences the political landscape even more than he did alive. So too Constance and Blanche may be peripheral rather than instrumental to political action, but both nonetheless give powerful voice to the tragedy of persons caught in and by the tides of historical necessity, more subject to the motions of others than mistresses of their own choices. Given that not only women and children but kings are so subject, their position is emblematic of the condition of all. The extravagant lament of Constance upon hearing that France has abandoned her cause expresses the frustration of almost every figure in this play when confronted by forces that mock personal agency: "O that my tongue were in the thunder's mouth!" (III.4.38). Blanche is perhaps the most poignant example of the way politics destroys the scope of private identity: offered as a bride to secure a treaty that is broken minutes after her marriage, she cries, "Which is the side that I must go withal? / I am with both. Each army hath a hand, / And in their rage, I having hold of both, / They whirl asunder and dismember me" (III.1.327-30).

The one figure who offers a resistance to the pressure of political circumstance upon personal agency is the Bastard. His very speech prefix announces his exclusion from a proper patrilineal authority; however, it is with that exclusion that his true power lies. In fact, it is an exclusion that he himself chooses when he renounces both his legitimacy and his inheritance in favor of a knighthood, a new name, and a claim to being the "reputed son of Coeur de Lion" (I.1.136). This renunciation is in itself a romantic act, and in a certain sense, a nonsensical one in the context of a medieval political world: to become "Lord of [his] presence and no land beside" (I.1.137), as Queen Eleanor puts it, or to claim "I am I, howe'er I was begot" (I.1.175) is to announce a kind of identity free of place and power and the usual terms of social identity. The Bastard embodies a kind of mobility unavailable to the other figures in this world: it is a freedom of social motion that sentimentally recalls the trajectory of the wandering knight, but combines it with the upstart energy of the self-invented man. Like Edmund in *King Lear,* also not begot betwixt the "lawful sheets," the Bastard claims along with his heritage a kind of audacious and improvisational vigor. His rowdy presence points a contrast not only with the unimpressive physical form of his brother but the immobilized and circumscribed figure of King John.

Along with this social mobility comes a verbal mobility; the Bastard performs as a kind of irreverent chorus, or even a Vice figure, expounding in soliloquy to the audience upon a variety of sociophilosophical themes: rank, "commodity," and the fickleness of kings' oaths when opportunity knocks – "Mad world! Mad kings! Mad composition!" (II.1.561). His is typically a cynical and demystifying voice, and he repeatedly declares to us his irreverence for social forms and his mercenary intentions: "Gain, be my lord, for I will worship thee!" (II.1.598). Ironically, however, the Bastard is perhaps the most loyal, and even sentimental, figure in the play. He avenges himself (and his supposed father) upon Austria; he orchestrates England's defense against France; and despite his avowed pragmatism he voices most clearly the outrage over Arthur's death: "From forth this morsel of dead royalty / The life, the right and truth of all this realm / Is fled to heaven, and England now is left / To tug and scramble" (IV.3.143-46). His self-possessed ambition to make power his goal notwithstanding, the Bastard also embodies that most impractical (and anachronistic) of sentiments: patriotic feeling. In a world where familiar international divisions apply only intermittently, where England lays claim to French territory, a French army defends the English throne, and Englishmen defect to the French, the Bastard has a refreshingly simple vision of geopolitical conflict: good guys (the English) and bad guys (everyone else). He closes the play with a couplet as sentimentally as it is metrically pat: "Nought shall make us rue / If England to itself do rest but true" (V.7.117-18). Even King John appears far more glorious in the Bastard's report than he does in his own person. His own decisions tend to be querulous, second-guessed, and ill-timed. He is at his most imperious when defying the pope and all his works, but it is a short-lived bravado, and his superstition increases in proportion to his political frailty. But to the Bastard, the king is – or at least could be, if he would just try – "warlike John; and in his forehead sits / A bare-ribbed death, whose office is this day / To feast upon whole thousands of the French" (V.2.176-78). The Bastard is as close to a popular hero as this play affords, and his voice is the sole locus of an inspirational national feeling.

King John, by contrast, cannot afford the luxury of either voicing or hearing such rhetoric. His title to the throne is under siege from the beginning, and whatever confidence in kingship he acquires by virtue of his victory over the combined forces of the church and the French is squandered by his decision to do away with his nephew and, with him, an alternative claim to the throne behind which perennially discontented nobles (a ubiquitous feature of Shakespeare's history plays) might rally. While in terms of practical politics this is perhaps the prudent choice, King John lacks the villainous brio of a Richard III (another nephew-killing king) to buoy him up: "I repent. / There is no sure foundation set on blood, / No certain life achieved by others' death" (IV.2.103-5). With his felt loss of moral confidence goes his political confidence: it seems not to even matter that Hubert frustrates his plans by sparing Arthur; practically speaking, it does not, since Arthur manages to kill himself in any case, and it proves in the end that a dead Arthur provokes as much dissent as a live one had. King John has too much of a conscience to be thoroughly bad, and yet his goodness is not timely or canny enough to be politically useful. As the play closes, he seems more and more himself to be carried along rudderless by the tide of events (much like his armies are "devourèd" by the Washes, V.6.41). His own image of himself is as a fragile text, "a scribbled form, drawn with a pen / Upon a parchment" (V.7.32–33), and like so many others in this world, he is more memorable in his pathos than his power.

CLAIRE MCEACHERN
University of California at Los Angeles

Note on the Text

THIS EDITION FOLLOWS closely the only substantive text of *King John,* that of the First Folio (1623). The folio text seems to have been set up from Shakespeare's own draft, possibly corrected before printing, particularly in the two final acts, by reference to the theater prompt copy. It is a fairly good text, but it shows some confusion and inconsistency in the names of characters in speech prefixes and stage directions. These have been corrected and regularized in the present edition, and a few additional emendations have been made, as listed below.

The following substantive departures, in italic type, have been made from the folio text. Some are readings from the Second (1632), Third (1663), or Fourth (1683) Folios; others are emendations made early in the history of Shakespearean scholarship and accepted by most modern editors. The authority for each is in parentheses, followed by the First Folio reading; both are in roman type.

I.1 147 *I would* (F2) It would   237 *Could he get me* (Vaughan) Could get me   257 *Thou art* (F4) That art
II.1 1 KING PHILIP (Theobald) Lewis   63 *Ate* (Rowe) Ace   109 *own* owe Ace   113 *breast* (F2) beast   144 *shows* (Theobald) shooes   149 *King Philip* (Theobald) King Lewis   150 KING PHILIP (Theobald) Lewis   200 **s.d.** *Enter . . . walls* (Oxford) Enter a Citizen upon the walles   215 *Confront* (Rowe) Comfort   259 *roundure* (Capell) rounder   335 *run* (F2) room   352 *dread* (Braunmuller, conj. Mull) dead   368 *Citizen* (Rowe) Fra.   371 *Kinged* (Tyrwhitt) Kings
III.1 74 **s.d.** *Enter . . . Austria* (Theobald) Enter . . . Austria, Constance   110 *day* (Theobald) daies   136 *God* (Braunmuller) heaven   148 *test* tast   155 *God* (Honigmann) heaven
III.3 *scene division* (Capell) [scene continues]   39 *ear* (Collier) race   52 *broad-eyed* (Pope) brooded
III.4 *scene division* (Capell) Scaena Tertia   44 *not holy* (F4) holy   48 *God* (Jowett) heaven   64 *friends* (Rowe) fiends
IV.1 23 *God* (Jowett) heaven   92 *mote* (Wilson) moth   123 *owns* owes

IV.2 1 *again* (F3) against   **42** *when* (Tyrwhitt) then   **73** *Does* (F4) Do
99 *owned* ow'd

IV.3 33 *man* (F2) mans   **41** *Have you* (F3) you have

V.2 26 *Were* (F2) Was   **36** *grapple* (Pope) cripple   **43** *hast thou* (F4) hast
135 *these* (Rowe) this

V.5 3 *measured* (Pope) measure

V.6 12 *eyeless* (Theobald) endless

V.7 17 *mind* (Rowe) winde   **21** *cygnet* (Rowe) Symet   **42** *strait* (Pope)
straight   **60** *God* (Honigmann, conj. Walker) heaven   **108** *give you
thanks* (Rowe) giue thankes

The Life and Death of
King John

[NAMES OF THE ACTORS

KING JOHN
PRINCE HENRY, *son to the king*
ARTHUR, *Duke of Bretagne (Brittany), nephew to the king*
THE EARL OF PEMBROKE
THE EARL OF ESSEX
THE EARL OF SALISBURY
THE LORD BIGOT
HUBERT DE BURGH
ROBERT FAULCONBRIDGE, *son to Sir Robert Faulconbridge*
PHILIP THE BASTARD, *his half brother*
JAMES GURNEY, *servant to Lady Faulconbridge*
PETER OF POMFRET, *a prophet*
PHILIP, *King of France*
LEWIS, *the Dauphin*
LIMOGES, *Duke of Austria*
CARDINAL PANDULPH, *the pope's representative*
MELUN, *a French lord*
CHATILLION, *ambassador from France*
QUEEN ELEANOR, *mother to King John*
CONSTANCE, *mother to Arthur*
BLANCHE OF SPAIN, *niece to King John*
LADY FAULCONBRIDGE
LORDS, LADIES, CITIZENS OF ANGIERS, SHERIFF, HERALDS, OFFICERS, SOLDIERS, EXECUTIONERS, MESSENGERS, AND OTHER ATTENDANTS

SCENE: *England and France*]

*

The Life and Death of King John

~ **I.1** *Enter King John, Queen Eleanor, Pembroke, Essex, and Salisbury, with the Chatillion of France.*

KING JOHN
  Now, say, Chatillion, what would France with us?
CHATILLION
  Thus, after greeting, speaks the King of France
  In my behavior to the majesty,   3
  The borrowed majesty, of England here.   4
ELEANOR
  A strange beginning: "borrowed majesty"!
KING JOHN
  Silence, good mother; hear the embassy.   6
CHATILLION
  Philip of France, in right and true behalf   7
  Of thy deceasèd brother Geoffrey's son,
  Arthur Plantagenet, lays most lawful claim
  To this fair island and the territories,   10
  To Ireland, Poitiers, Anjou, Touraine, Maine,
  Desiring thee to lay aside the sword   12

I.1 The English court   **3** *In my behavior* through my person   **4** *borrowed majesty* stolen sovereignty; *England* i.e., King John   **6** *embassy* message
7 *Philip of France* Philip II (1165–1223); *in right and true behalf* in support of the lawful claim   **10** *the territories* feudal lands owing sovereignty to the English crown   **12** *the sword* i.e., of state

13 Which sways usurpingly these several titles,
    And put the same into young Arthur's hand,
    Thy nephew and right royal sovereign.

KING JOHN

16 What follows if we disallow of this?

CHATILLION

17 The proud control of fierce and bloody war,
    To enforce these rights so forcibly withheld.

KING JOHN

19 Here have we war for war and blood for blood,
20 Controlment for controlment; so answer France.

CHATILLION

    Then take my king's defiance from my mouth,
22 The farthest limit of my embassy.

KING JOHN

    Bear mine to him, and so depart in peace.
    Be thou as lightning in the eyes of France,
25 For, ere thou canst report, I will be there.
26 The thunder of my cannon shall be heard.
27 So, hence! Be thou the trumpet of our wrath
28 And sullen presage of your own decay.
29 An honorable conduct let him have;
30 Pembroke, look to't. Farewell, Chatillion.
                            Exit Chatillion and Pembroke.

ELEANOR

31 What now, my son! Have I not ever said
    How that ambitious Constance would not cease
33 Till she had kindled France and all the world
34 Upon the right and party of her son?

---

13 *usurpingly* unlawfully, presumptuously   16 *disallow of* refuse   17 *control* enforcement   19 *Here* (1) in England, (2) in response   20 *Controlment* compulsion   22 *The . . . embassy* the full and / or furthest extent of my charge as messenger   25 *ere* before; *report* deliver your message (with secondary meaning of thunder)   26 *cannon* (an anachronism, since gunpowder had not yet been invented)   27 *trumpet* (as a herald)   28 *sullen presage* somber prophecy; *decay* destruction   29 *conduct* escort   31 *ever* always   33 *France* i.e., French king and / or French nation   34 *party* behalf

This might have been prevented and made whole   35
With very easy arguments of love,   36
Which now the manage of two kingdoms must   37
With fearful bloody issue arbitrate.   38

KING JOHN
Our strong possession and our right for us.   39

ELEANOR
Your strong possession much more than your right,   40
Or else it must go wrong with you and me –
So much my conscience whispers in your ear,
Which none but heaven, and you, and I, shall hear.
          Enter a Sheriff [who speaks aside to Essex].

ESSEX
My liege, here is the strangest controversy,
Come from the country to be judged by you,   45
That e'er I heard. Shall I produce the men?

KING JOHN
Let them approach.
Our abbeys and our priories shall pay
This expeditious charge.   49
          *Enter Robert Faulconbridge, and Philip [his bastard
          brother].*
                              What men are you?

BASTARD
Your faithful subject, I, a gentleman,   50
Born in Northamptonshire, and eldest son,
As I suppose, to Robert Faulconbridge,
A soldier, by the honor-giving hand
Of Coeur de Lion knighted in the field.   54

KING JOHN   *[To Robert]*
What art thou?

---

35 *made whole* patched up, remedied   **36** *arguments of love* (1) expressions of
affection, (2) friendly discussions   **37** *manage* government   **38** *issue* results
39 *for us* on our side   **45** *the country* i.e., the provinces   **49** *expeditious*
speedy, sudden   **54** *Coeur de Lion* i.e., Richard the Lionhearted, King
Richard I

ROBERT
> The son and heir to that same Faulconbridge.

KING JOHN
> Is that the elder, and art thou the heir?
> You came not of one mother then, it seems.

BASTARD
> Most certain of one mother, mighty king;
60 > That is well known; and, as I think, one father.
> But for the certain knowledge of that truth
62 > I put you o'er to heaven and to my mother.
63 > Of that I doubt, as all men's children may.

ELEANOR
64 > Out on thee, rude man! Thou dost shame thy mother
65 > And wound her honor with this diffidence.

BASTARD
> I, madam? No, I have no reason for it;
> That is my brother's plea and none of mine;
68 > The which if he can prove, a pops me out
69 > At least from fair five hundred pound a year.
70 > Heaven guard my mother's honor and my land!

KING JOHN
> A good blunt fellow. Why, being younger born,
> Doth he lay claim to thine inheritance?

BASTARD
> I know not why, except to get the land.
74 > But once he slandered me with bastardy.
75 > But whe'r I be as true begot or no,
76 > That still I lay upon my mother's head;
> But that I am as well begot, my liege –
78 > Fair fall the bones that took the pains for me –

---

62 *put you o'er* refer you   **63** *that* i.e., that truth (of his paternity)   **64** *Out on thee* Get away! Get out!   **65** *diffidence* distrust   **68** *a* he; *pops me out* ejects me from, cuts me out of   **69** *fair* fully, at least   **74** *once* on a single occasion, which he dare not repeat   **75** *whe'r* whether; *true begot* legitimately conceived   **76** *lay . . . head* let my mother account for   **78** *Fair . . . me* May good befall the person who took the trouble to conceive me (perhaps with a pun on the "fallen" woman, his mother)

Compare our faces and be judge yourself.
If old Sir Robert did beget us both,   80
And were our father, and this son like him,
O old Sir Robert, father, on my knee
I give heaven thanks I was not like to thee!   83

KING JOHN
Why, what a madcap hath heaven lent us here!   84

ELEANOR
He hath a trick of Coeur de Lion's face;   85
The accent of his tongue affecteth him.   86
Do you not read some tokens of my son
In the large composition of this man?   88

KING JOHN
Mine eye hath well examinèd his parts,
And finds them perfect Richard. Sirrah, speak.   90
What doth move you to claim your brother's land?

BASTARD
Because he hath a half-face like my father.   92
With half that face would he have all my land –
A half-faced groat five hundred pound a year!   94

ROBERT
My gracious liege, when that my father lived,
Your brother did employ my father much –

BASTARD
Well, sir, by this you cannot get my land.
Your tale must be how he employed my mother.   98

ROBERT
And once dispatched him in an embassy   99
To Germany, there with the emperor   100
To treat of high affairs touching that time.   101

---

83 *like to* resembling   84 *madcap* crazy rascal   85 *trick* characteristic expression   86 *accent of his tongue* sound of his voice; *affecteth* resembles   88 *large composition* big build (Richard I was reputed to be a large man)   90 *perfect* exactly, like to   92 *half-face* profile (with secondary meaning of imperfect)   94 *half-faced groat* a thin silver coin with a profile stamped upon it   98 *employed* used (implying sexual relations)   99 *dispatched* sent; *in* on   101 *treat* deal with; *high* important

Th' advantage of his absence took the king,
103 And in the mean time sojourned at my father's;
104 Where how he did prevail I shame to speak,
But truth is truth; large lengths of seas and shores
Between my father and my mother lay,
As I have heard my father speak himself,
108 When this same lusty gentleman was got.
Upon his deathbed he by will bequeathed
110 His lands to me, and took it on his death
That this my mother's son was none of his;
And if he were, he came into the world
113 Full fourteen weeks before the course of time.
Then, good my liege, let me have what is mine,
My father's land, as was my father's will.

KING JOHN
Sirrah, your brother is legitimate.
Your father's wife did after wedlock bear him,
118 And if she did play false, the fault was hers,
119 Which fault lies on the hazards of all husbands
120 That marry wives. Tell me, how if my brother,
Who, as you say, took pains to get this son,
Had of your father claimed this son for his?
123 In sooth, good friend, your father might have kept
124 This calf, bred from his cow, from all the world.
125 In sooth he might; then, if he were my brother's,
My brother might not claim him, nor your father,
127 Being none of his, refuse him. This concludes;

---

103 *mean* intervening; *sojourned at* stayed with   104 *shame* am ashamed
108 *lusty* merry; *got* conceived   110 *took it on his death* swore on his
deathbed (the most solemn kind of oath)   113 *course of time* due date of
full-term pregnancy   118 *play false* commit adultery   119 *fault* (1) error,
(2) vagina; *lies on the hazards* is one of the risks   123 *sooth* truth   124
from . . . world for himself (e.g., the owner of a cow also owns the offspring,
no matter who owns the sire)   125–27 *then . . . him* if Philip Faulconbridge
were Richard I's son, Richard I could not claim him as his own, nor could
your father, even if he knew Philip not to be his own son, legally disown him
127 *refuse* disclaim; *concludes* settles the question decisively

My mother's son did get your father's heir;
Your father's heir must have your father's land.

ROBERT
Shall then my father's will be of no force   130
To dispossess that child which is not his?

BASTARD
Of no more force to dispossess me, sir,
Than was his will to get me, as I think.   133

ELEANOR
Whether hadst thou rather be a Faulconbridge,   134
And like thy brother, to enjoy thy land,   135
Or the reputed son of Coeur de Lion,   136
Lord of thy presence and no land beside?   137

BASTARD
Madam, and if my brother had my shape
And I had his, Sir Robert's his, like him,   139
And if my legs were two such riding rods,   140
My arms such eelskins stuffed, my face so thin
That in mine ear I durst not stick a rose   142
Lest men should say, "Look, where three farthings goes!"
And, to his shape, were heir to all this land,   144
Would I might never stir from off this place,
I would give it every foot to have this face;   146
I would not be Sir Nob in any case.   147

ELEANOR
I like thee well. Wilt thou forsake thy fortune,

---

130 *will* last testament; intention **133** *will* (1) intention, (2) lust, (3) penis
134 *Whether . . . be* which would you rather be **135** *like thy brother* i.e., in
physical appearance (being of the same father), and therefore **136** *reputed*
supposed **137** *presence* own person **139** *Sir Robert's his* i.e., his father's
shape **140** *riding rods* short whips (i.e., scrawny, as are *eelskins stuffed*)
142–43 *ear . . . goes* (certain coins were distinguished from others by a rose
behind Queen Elizabeth's head; he is saying that his brother dare not place a
rose behind his ear, as a lover might, lest he be taken for a three-farthing
piece, his face being so thin) **144** *to* in **146** *it* i.e., the land; *every foot* every
foot of it; *this* i.e., my own **147** *Sir Nob* (1) a demeaning nickname for
"Robert," (2) with a pun on "knob" – i.e., one with a knob for a head (on a
skinny body), (3) simpleton; *in any case* for anything

Bequeath thy land to him, and follow me?
150 I am a soldier and now bound to France.

BASTARD
Brother, take you my land, I'll take my chance.
Your face hath got five hundred pound a year,
153 Yet sell your face for fivepence and 'tis dear.
Madam, I'll follow you unto the death.

ELEANOR
155 Nay, I would have you go before me thither.

BASTARD
156 Our country manners give our betters way.

KING JOHN
What is thy name?

BASTARD
Philip, my liege, so is my name begun;
Philip, good old Sir Robert's wife's eldest son.

KING JOHN
160 From henceforth bear his name whose form thou bearest.
161 Kneel thou down Philip, but rise more great;
162 Arise Sir Richard, and Plantagenet.

BASTARD
Brother by th' mother's side, give me your hand.
My father gave me honor, yours gave land.
165 Now blessèd be the hour, by night or day,
166 When I was got, Sir Robert was away!

ELEANOR
The very spirit of Plantagenet!
168 I am thy grandam, Richard; call me so.

---

150 *to* for   153 *'tis dear* too costly   155 *go before me thither* precede me to
France (or to death?)   156 *country . . . way* rustic or provincial customs decree that we give way to our social superiors   160 *form* shape, likeness   161
great i.e., of higher rank   162 *Plantagenet* i.e., the family name of King
Richard (and John himself)   165 *hour* (with a possible pun on "whore,"
since both words were pronounced identically)   166 *got* conceived   168
grandam grandmother

BASTARD

    Madam, by chance but not by truth; what though?   169

    Something about a little from the right,   170

    In at the window, or else o'er the hatch: 171

    Who dares not stir by day must walk by night,

    And have is have, however men do catch.   173

    Near or far off, well won is still well shot,   174

    And I am I, howe'er I was begot.

KING JOHN

    Go, Faulconbridge. Now hast thou thy desire;

    A landless knight makes thee a landed squire.   177

    Come, madam, and come, Richard, we must speed

    For France, for France, for it is more than need.   179

BASTARD

    Brother, adieu; good fortune come to thee!   *180*

    For thou wast got i' th' way of honesty.

                        Exeunt all but Bastard.

    A foot of honor better than I was,   182

    But many a many foot of land the worse.

    Well, now can I make any Joan a lady.   184

    "Good den, Sir Richard!" – "God-a-mercy, fellow" –   185

    And if his name be George, I'll call him Peter,

    For new-made honor doth forget men's names;   187

    'Tis too respective and too sociable   188

    For your conversion. Now your traveler,   189

---

169 *by . . . truth* by accident if not by honesty (of conduct); *what though* so what   **170** *about* near   **171** *In . . . hatch* (proverbial expressions referring to illegitimate birth)   **173** *have . . . catch* i.e., possession is nine tenths of the law, however one gains it   **174** *Near . . . shot* however far away the target, the archer still deserves credit for hitting it (with sexual innuendo: *won* = seduced; *shot* = performed sexually)   **177** *landless knight* i.e., the bastard (who has just renounced his land in favor of his brother); *squire* (a rank below knight)   **179** *it . . . need* it is extremely pressing, more than necessary   **182** *foot* step   **184** *Joan* (name used for any girl of lowly station)   **185** *Good den* God give you good even; *God-a-mercy* God reward you   **187** *new-made honor* recently ennobled (and thus pretentiously snobbish toward others)   **188** *respective* respectful, courteous   **189** *conversion* change of status

190   He and his toothpick at my worship's mess,
191   And when my knightly stomach is sufficed,
192   Why then I suck my teeth and catechize
193   My pickèd man of countries: "My dear sir" –
          Thus, leaning on mine elbow, I begin –
          "I shall beseech you" – that is question now;
196   And then comes answer like an Absey book;
          "O, sir," says answer, "at your best command,
          At your employment, at your service, sir";
          "No, sir," says question, "I, sweet sir, at yours";
200   And so, ere answer knows what question would,
201   Saving in dialogue of compliment,
202   And talking of the Alps and Apennines,
          The Pyrenean and the river Po,
204   It draws toward supper in conclusion so.
205   But this is worshipful society,
206   And fits the mounting spirit like myself,
207   For he is but a bastard to the time
208   That doth not smack of observation.
          And so am I, whether I smack or no,
210   And not alone in habit and device,
211   Exterior form, outward accoutrement,
212   But from the inward motion to deliver
213   Sweet, sweet, sweet poison for the age's tooth,

---

190 *toothpick* (a sign of affectation, associated particularly with the foreign traveler); *my worship's mess* my own lordly dinner table   191 *sufficed* satisfied 192 *suck my teeth* i.e., suck on my teeth; *catechize* interrogate in a question-and-answer format   193 *pickèd* (1) refined, rarefied, (2) whose teeth have been picked; *of countries* about foreign lands   196 *Absey book* ABC book, primer for instruction of children (the Bastard is mimicking the kind of exercise found in such books)   201 *Saving in* except in; *dialogue of compliment* formal, elegant address   202 *Alps and Apennines* i.e., foreign places   204 *It . . . supper* suppertime draws near   205 *worshipful society* sophisticated (and snobbish) company or conversation   206 *mounting spirit* ambitious soul   207 *bastard to the time* no true son of the age   208 *smack* have the air of; *observation* (1) obsequiousness, servility, (2) noticing   210 *alone* only; *habit* dress; *device* heraldic figure or emblem   211 *accoutrement* clothing 212 *But . . . motion* also from within my behavior   213 *Sweet . . . poison* flattery

Which, though I will not practice to deceive,   214
Yet, to avoid deceit, I mean to learn;   215
For it shall strew the footsteps of my rising.   216
But who comes in such haste in riding robes?
What woman-post is this? Hath she no husband   218
That will take pains to blow a horn before her?   219
    Enter Lady Faulconbridge and James Gurney.
O me! 'Tis my mother. How now, good lady!   220
What brings you here to court so hastily?

LADY FAULCONBRIDGE
Where is that slave, thy brother? Where is he,
That holds in chase mine honor up and down?   223

BASTARD
My brother Robert? Old Sir Robert's son?
Colbrand the giant, that same mighty man?   225
Is it Sir Robert's son that you seek so?

LADY FAULCONBRIDGE
Sir Robert's son! Ay, thou unreverent boy,   227
Sir Robert's son! Why scorn'st thou at Sir Robert?
He is Sir Robert's son, and so art thou.

BASTARD
James Gurney, wilt thou give us leave awhile?   230

GURNEY
Good leave, good Philip.   231

BASTARD   Philip sparrow! James,
There's toys abroad; anon I'll tell thee more.   232
                                    Exit James.
Madam, I was not old Sir Robert's son.

---

214 *practice* explicitly endeavor **215** *deceit* being deceived **216** *it . . . rising* i.e., flattery will accompany his rise to greatness as rushes are strewn upon a great man's floor **218** *woman-post* female courier **219** *blow a horn* i.e., announce his cuckoldry and her infidelity (cuckolds were thought to grow horns, and unaccompanied women were thought unchaste) **223** *holds in chase* pursues to destroy **225** *Colbrand* a Danish giant killed by Guy of Warwick in the old romance **227** *unreverent* impertinent **230** *give us leave* excuse us **231** *Philip sparrow* (since he has just been knighted, he objects to being called merely Philip, the common name for a sparrow) **232** *toys abroad* strange doings afoot

234   Sir Robert might have eat his part in me
       Upon Good Friday and ne'er broke his fast.
236   Sir Robert could do well – marry, to confess –
       Could he get me! Sir Robert could not do it.
238   We know his handiwork. Therefore, good mother,
239   To whom am I beholden for these limbs?
240   Sir Robert never holp to make this leg.

LADY FAULCONBRIDGE
       Hast thou conspirèd with thy brother too,
242   That for thine own gain shouldst defend mine honor?
243   What means this scorn, thou most untoward knave?

BASTARD
244   Knight, knight, good mother, Basilisco-like.
245   What! I am dubbed; I have it on my shoulder.
       But, mother, I am not Sir Robert's son;
       I have disclaimed Sir Robert and my land;
       Legitimation, name, and all is gone.
       Then, good my mother, let me know my father;
250   Some proper man I hope; who was it, mother?

LADY FAULCONBRIDGE
251   Hast thou denied thyself a Faulconbridge?

BASTARD
       As faithfully as I deny the devil.

LADY FAULCONBRIDGE
       King Richard Coeur de Lion was thy father.
254   By long and vehement suit I was seduced
       To make room for him in my husband's bed.

234–35 *eat his part . . . fast* (a turn on a proverbial phrase, meaning that Sir Robert had no part in his conception)   236–37 *Sir Robert . . . get me* (he is incredulous at the suggestion that one like Sir Robert might be his father)   238 *handiwork* i.e., type of offspring (his scrawny brother)   239 *beholden* indebted   240 *holp* helped   242 *That . . . honor* that for your own good should protect my good reputation   243 *untoward* ill-mannered   244 *Basilisco-like* (the Bastard mocks himself by comparing himself to Basilisco, the cowardly, braggart knight in *Soliman and Perseda,* an old play probably by Thomas Kyd)   245 *dubbed* made a knight   250 *proper* handsome   251 *denied thyself* i.e., renounced your Faulconbridge heritage   254 *suit* entreaty

Heaven lay not my transgression to my charge!   256
Thou art the issue of my dear offense,   257
Which was so strongly urged past my defense.   258

BASTARD

Now, by this light, were I to get again,   259
Madam, I would not wish a better father.   260
Some sins do bear their privilege on earth,   261
And so doth yours; your fault was not your folly.
Needs must you lay your heart at his dispose,   263
Subjected tribute to commanding love,   264
Against whose fury and unmatchèd force
The aweless lion could not wage the fight,   266
Nor keep his princely heart from Richard's hand.
He that perforce robs lions of their hearts   268
May easily win a woman's. Ay, my mother,
With all my heart I thank thee for my father!   270
Who lives and dares but say thou didst not well
When I was got, I'll send his soul to hell.
Come, lady, I will show thee to my kin,
And they shall say, when Richard me begot,
If thou hadst said him nay, it had been sin.   275
Who says it was, he lies; I say 'twas not.   *Exeunt.*

＊

---

256 *lay . . . charge* blame me for my fault   257 *issue* result; *dear* (1) costly,
(2) cherished   258 *urged . . . defense* forced in spite of my protests   259 *get*
be conceived   261 *do bear . . . earth* are allowed on earth but not in heaven
263 *Needs . . . dispose* you had to yield your body to his use   264 *Subjected*
subservient or obedient   266 *aweless lion* (King Richard, according to leg-
end, had slain a lion by thrusting his hand down its throat and tearing out its
heart, which he then ate; hence his nickname)   268 *perforce* forcibly   275
said him nay refused him

∾ **II.1** *Enter before Angiers, Philip King of France,*
Lewis [the] Dauphin, Austria, Constance, Arthur
[, and Attendants].

KING PHILIP

Before Angiers well met, brave Austria.

2   Arthur, that great forerunner of thy blood,

Richard, that robbed the lion of his heart

4   And fought the holy wars in Palestine,

5   By this brave duke came early to his grave;

6   And for amends to his posterity,

7   At our importance hither is he come

8   To spread his colors, boy, in thy behalf,

And to rebuke the usurpation

10   Of thy unnatural uncle, English John.

Embrace him, love him, give him welcome hither.

ARTHUR

God shall forgive you Coeur de Lion's death

13   The rather that you give his offspring life,

14   Shadowing their right under your wings of war.

I give you welcome with a powerless hand,

But with a heart full of unstainèd love.

Welcome before the gates of Angiers, duke.

LEWIS

18   A noble boy! Who would not do thee right?

AUSTRIA

Upon thy cheek lay I this zealous kiss,

II.1 Angiers   **2** *forerunner of thy blood* ancestor (Arthur was actually the
nephew of Richard, son of his brother Geoffrey)   **4** *holy wars* the Christian
Crusades   **5** *brave duke* Austria (although Richard actually was killed before
the castle of the Viscount of Limoges, Shakespeare, following his source,
combines the two characters)   **6** *to his posterity* (1) for his descendants, (2)
for his future rewards, either heavenly or political   **7** *importance* request   **8**
spread his colors (1) display his flag, (2) show his allegiance   **10** *unnatural*
i.e., because usurping   **13** *The rather* because; *offspring* descendant, heir   **14**
Shadowing sheltering   **18** *do thee right* i.e., do right by you

As seal to this indenture of my love,   20
That to my home I will no more return
Till Angiers and the right thou hast in France,
Together with that pale, that white-faced shore,   23
Whose foot spurns back the ocean's roaring tides   24
And coops from other lands her islanders,   25
Even till that England, hedged in with the main,   26
That water-wallèd bulwark, still secure   27
And confident from foreign purposes,   28
Even till that utmost corner of the west
Salute thee for her king. Till then, fair boy,   30
Will I not think of home, but follow arms.   31

CONSTANCE
O, take his mother's thanks, a widow's thanks,
Till your strong hand shall help to give him strength
To make a more requital to your love.   34

AUSTRIA
The peace of heaven is theirs that lift their swords
In such a just and charitable war.

KING PHILIP
Well then, to work; our cannon shall be bent   37
Against the brows of this resisting town.   38
Call for our chiefest men of discipline,   39
To cull the plots of best advantages.   40
We'll lay before this town our royal bones,
Wade to the marketplace in Frenchmen's blood,
But we will make it subject to this boy.

CONSTANCE
Stay for an answer to your embassy,   44

---

20 *indenture* sealed contract   **23** *pale . . . shore* the white cliffs of the south-eastern English coast   **24** *spurns back* repels   **25** *coops* encloses for protection   **26** *main* ocean   **27** *still* forever   **28** *confident* secure; *purposes* designs   **31** *follow arms* pursue warfare   **34** *more requital* greater thanks, return   **37** *bent* directed   **38** *Against the brows* i.e., at the boundaries (the forehead)   **39** *discipline* military training or experience   **40** *cull . . . advantages* select the most suitable locations for placing cannons   **44** *Stay* wait

45   Lest unadvised you stain your swords with blood.
      My Lord Chatillion may from England bring
      That right in peace which here we urge in war,
      And then we shall repent each drop of blood
49   That hot rash haste so indirectly shed.
           Enter Chatillion.

KING PHILIP

50   A wonder, lady! Lo, upon thy wish,
      Our messenger, Chatillion, is arrived!
52   What England says, say briefly, gentle lord;
53   We coldly pause for thee; Chatillion, speak.

CHATILLION

      Then turn your forces from this paltry siege
55   And stir them up against a mightier task.
56   England, impatient of your just demands,
      Hath put himself in arms. The adverse winds,
58   Whose leisure I have stayed, have given him time
      To land his legions all as soon as I.
60   His marches are expedient to this town,
      His forces strong, his soldiers confident.
      With him along is come the mother queen,
63   An Ate, stirring him to blood and strife;
      With her her niece, the Lady Blanche of Spain;
65   With them a bastard of the king's deceased;
66   And all th' unsettled humors of the land,
67   Rash, inconsiderate, fiery voluntaries,
68   With ladies' faces and fierce dragons' spleens,
      Have sold their fortunes at their native homes,

---

45 *unadvised* unwisely, without adequate consideration   49 *indirectly* point-
lessly 52 *England* King John 53 *coldly* calmly 55 *stir them up* rouse
them; *against* toward 56 *impatient of* provoked by 58 *leisure . . . stayed* for
whose cessation I have awaited 60 *marches* marching forces; *expedient to*
hastening toward 63 *Ate* the Greek goddess of mischief and vengeance 65
of . . . deceased of the late king 66 *unsettled humors* restless disgruntled men
67 *voluntaries* volunteers 68 *ladies' faces* i.e., good-looking; *dragons' spleens*
hot tempers (since the spleen was regarded as the seat of the passions)

Bearing their birthrights proudly on their backs,   70
To make a hazard of new fortunes here.   71
In brief, a braver choice of dauntless spirits   72
Than now the English bottoms have waft o'er   73
Did never float upon the swelling tide,
To do offense and scathe in Christendom.   75
The interruption of their churlish drums   76
Cuts off more circumstance; they are at hand.   77
      Drum beats.
To parley or to fight, therefore prepare.   78

KING PHILIP
How much unlooked for is this expedition!   79

AUSTRIA
By how much unexpected, by so much   80
We must awake endeavor for defense,   81
For courage mounteth with occasion.   82
Let them be welcome then; we are prepared.
      Enter King [John] of England, Bastard, Queen
      [Eleanor], Blanche, Pembroke, and others.

KING JOHN
Peace be to France, if France in peace permit
Our just and lineal entrance to our own.   85
If not, bleed France, and peace ascend to heaven,
Whiles we, God's wrathful agent, do correct   87
Their proud contempt that beats his peace to heaven.

KING PHILIP
Peace be to England, if that war return   89
From France to England, there to live in peace.   90

---

70 *Bearing . . . backs* having sold their estates to purchase armor   **71** *make a hazard of* take a chance on   **72** *In brief* in short; *braver* more splendid, worthier   **73** *bottoms* ships   **75** *scathe* harm   **76** *churlish* lowly, inferior   **77** *Cuts off* prohibits, cuts short; *circumstance* details   **78** *parley* negotiate   **79** *expedition* (1) army, (2) haste   **81** *awake endeavor* rouse our efforts   **82** *occasion* cause   **85** *lineal* legitimate (because duly inherited)   **87** *God's . . . agent* (John describes himself and his army as a divine scourge for [French] sins); *correct* punish   **89** *if that* if

91 England we love, and for that England's sake
    With burden of our armor here we sweat.
93 This toil of ours should be a work of thine,
    But thou from loving England art so far
95 That thou hast underwrought his lawful king,
96 Cut off the sequence of posterity,
97 Outfacèd infant state, and done a rape
    Upon the maiden virtue of the crown.
    Look here upon thy brother Geoffrey's face.
100 These eyes, these brows, were molded out of his;
101 This little abstract doth contain that large
    Which died in Geoffrey, and the hand of time
103 Shall draw this brief into as huge a volume.
    That Geoffrey was thy elder brother born,
    And this his son. England was Geoffrey's right
106 And this is Geoffrey's in the name of God.
    How comes it then that thou art called a king,
108 When living blood doth in these temples beat,
109 Which own the crown that thou o'ermasterest?

KING JOHN

110 From whom hast thou this great commission, France,
111 To draw my answer from thy articles?

KING PHILIP

112 From that supernal judge that stirs good thoughts
    In any breast of strong authority,

---

91 *England's* i.e., Arthur's (since Philip takes him to be the lawful king of England)   **93** *This toil . . . thine* i.e., John should be fighting for Arthur's cause rather than against him   **95** *underwrought* undermined   **96** *sequence of posterity* hereditary succession to the throne   **97** *Outfacèd infant state* intimidated a child king   **101–3** *little abstract . . . volume* i.e., Arthur as a child is like a shortened edition of his father, Geoffrey, but in time he will grow to be as complete a volume (of virtues) as his father was   **103** *brief* note, sketch (i.e., Arthur, and his legal claim)   **106** *this* (a famous crux; may refer to Arthur, John's crown, or the city of Angiers, depending upon what the actor indicates by his arm)   **108** *these* i.e., Arthur's   **109** *o'ermasterest* overpower, usurp   **110** *commission* responsibility, charge   **111** *draw . . . articles* demand that I answer your charges   **112** *supernal* heavenly

To look into the blots and stains of right.   114
That judge hath made me guardian to this boy,
Under whose warrant I impeach thy wrong   116
And by whose help I mean to chastise it.

KING JOHN
Alack, thou dost usurp authority.

KING PHILIP
Excuse it is to beat usurping down.

ELEANOR
Who is it thou dost call usurper, France?   120

CONSTANCE
Let me make answer: thy usurping son.

ELEANOR
Out, insolent! Thy bastard shall be king
That thou mayst be a queen and check the world!   123

CONSTANCE
My bed was ever to thy son as true
As thine was to thy husband, and this boy
Liker in feature to his father Geoffrey
Than thou and John, in manners being as like
As rain to water, or devil to his dam.   128
My boy a bastard! By my soul I think
His father never was so true begot.   130
It cannot be and if thou wert his mother.   131

ELEANOR
There's a good mother, boy, that blots thy father.   132

CONSTANCE
There's a good grandam, boy, that would blot thee.   133

---

114 *blots and stains* injuries (the image sustains the operative metaphor of legal document)   116 *impeach* accuse   123 *queen* (with play on "quean," whore); *check* control (with possible allusion to the game of chess)   128 *dam* mother   131 *and if* if   132 *blots* slanders   133 *grandam* grandmother

AUSTRIA

134   Peace!

BASTARD   Hear the crier.

AUSTRIA   What the devil art thou?

BASTARD

    One that will play the devil, sir, with you,

136   An a may catch your hide and you alone.

137   You are the hare of whom the proverb goes,

    Whose valor plucks dead lions by the beard.

139   I'll smoke your skin coat, an I catch you right.

140   Sirrah, look to 't; i' faith, I will, i' faith.

BLANCHE

141   O well did he become that lion's robe,

    That did disrobe the lion of that robe!

BASTARD

143   It lies as sightly on the back of him

144   As great Alcides' shows upon an ass.

    But, ass, I'll take that burden from your back,

146   Or lay on that shall make your shoulders crack.

AUSTRIA

147   What cracker is this same that deafs our ears

    With this abundance of superfluous breath?

149   King Philip, determine what we shall do straight.

KING PHILIP

150   Women and fools, break off your conference.

    King John, this is the very sum of all:

152   England and Ireland, Angiers, Touraine, Maine,

    In right of Arthur do I claim of thee.

---

134 *Hear the crier* (the Bastard mocks Austria by likening him to the town crier who called for silence in the courts)   **136** *An a* if he; *catch your hide* punish you (the Bastard perhaps refers to a lion skin worn by Austria and formerly belonging to Richard I)   **137** *the proverb* i.e., "hares may pull dead lions by the beard" (it occurs in the *Adagia* of Erasmus)   **139** *smoke your skin coat* thrash you   **141** *become* wear well, was suited to   **143** *sightly* appropriately; *him* i.e., Austria   **144** *Alcides* Hercules, who wore the skin of the Nemean lion he had slain   **146** *lay on* i.e., deliver blows   **147** *cracker* boaster; *deafs* deafens   **149** *straight* immediately   **150** *fools* children; *conference* discussion, squabbling   **152** *Angiers* (here confused with Anjou)

Wilt thou resign them and lay down thy arms?

KING JOHN
My life as soon! I do defy thee, France.
Arthur of Bretagne, yield thee to my hand,
And out of my dear love I'll give thee more
Than e'er the coward hand of France can win.
Submit thee, boy.

ELEANOR   Come to thy grandam, child.

CONSTANCE
Do, child, go to it grandam, child;   160
Give grandam kingdom, and it grandam will   161
Give it a plum, a cherry, and a fig.   162
There's a good grandam.

ARTHUR   Good my mother, peace!
I would that I were low laid in my grave.
I am not worth this coil that's made for me.   165

ELEANOR
His mother shames him so, poor boy, he weeps.   166

CONSTANCE
Now shame upon you, whe'r she does or no!   167
His grandam's wrongs, and not his mother's shames,
Draws those heaven-moving pearls from his poor eyes,   169
Which heaven shall take in nature of a fee.   170
Ay, with these crystal beads heaven shall be bribed   171
To do him justice and revenge on you.

ELEANOR
Thou monstrous slanderer of heaven and earth!

CONSTANCE
Thou monstrous injurer of heaven and earth!
Call not me slanderer; thou and thine usurp
The dominations, royalties, and rights   176

160–63 *Do . . . grandam* (Constance uses baby talk to ridicule Eleanor's invitation) 161 *it* its 162 *fig* (1) poisoned fruit, (2) obscene gesture, (3) a small and worthless item 165 *coil* fuss 166 *shames* embarrasses, disgraces 167 *whe'r* whether 169 *Draws* draw; *pearls* tears 170 *fee* legal fee 171 *beads* (1) tears, (2) rosary beads 176 *dominations* sovereignties

177   Of this oppressèd boy. This is thy eldest son's son,
178   Infortunate in nothing but in thee.
179   Thy sins are visited in this poor child;
180   The canon of the law is laid on him,
       Being but the second generation
182   Removèd from thy sin-conceiving womb.

KING JOHN
183   Bedlam, have done.

CONSTANCE   I have but this to say,
184   That he is not only plaguèd for her sin,
       But God hath made her sin and her the plague
186   On this removèd issue, plagued for her
       And with her plague; her sin his injury,
188   Her injury the beadle to her sin,
       All punished in the person of this child,
190   And all for her; a plague upon her.

ELEANOR
191   Thou unadvisèd scold, I can produce
192   A will that bars the title of thy son.

CONSTANCE
       Ay, who doubts that? A will! A wicked will;
194   A woman's will; a cankered grandam's will!

KING PHILIP
195   Peace, lady! Pause, or be more temperate.
196   It ill beseems this presence to cry aim

---

177 *eldest son's son* oldest grandson (a biblical form; not son of your oldest son, which Arthur was not)   178 *Infortunate* unfortunate   179 *visited* punished   180 *canon of the law* i.e., that the sins of parents be visited upon their children to the third and fourth generation   182 *Removèd* distant (at two generational removes)   183 *Bedlam* lunatic   184–90 *That . . . upon her* (a perhaps intentionally obscure passage, the sense being that Arthur is being punished for the sin of Eleanor – her giving birth to John, whom Constance is calling a bastard – by the very presence of Eleanor and John, that they are laying the scourge upon him that should be laid upon Eleanor)   186 *removèd issue* distant descendant   188 *beadle* a parish official who meted out corporal punishment, to prostitutes in particular   191 *unadvisèd* rash   192 *A will* (the last testament of King Richard I, which named his brother John heir to the throne)   194 *cankered* malignant   195 *temperate* calm   196 *cry aim* give encouragement

To these ill-tunèd repetitions.
Some trumpet summon hither to the walls   198
These men of Angiers. Let us hear them speak
Whose title they admit, Arthur's or John's.   200
    Trumpet sounds. Enter Citizen[s] [of
    Angiers, including Hubert,] upon the walls.
CITIZEN
    Who is it that hath warned us to the walls?   201
KING PHILIP
    'Tis France, for England.
KING JOHN   England for itself.
    You men of Angiers, and my loving subjects –
KING PHILIP
    You loving men of Angiers, Arthur's subjects,
    Our trumpet called you to this gentle parle –   205
KING JOHN
    For our advantage; therefore hear us first.
    These flags of France, that are advancèd here   207
    Before the eye and prospect of your town,   208
    Have hither marched to your endamagement.   209
    The cannons have their bowels full of wrath,   210
    And ready mounted are they to spit forth
    Their iron indignation 'gainst your walls.
    All preparation for a bloody siege
    And merciless proceeding by these French
    Confront your city's eyes, your winking gates,   215
    And but for our approach those sleeping stones,   216
    That as a waist doth girdle you about,   217
    By the compulsion of their ordinance   218
    By this time from their fixèd beds of lime   219
    Had been dishabited, and wide havoc made   220
    For bloody power to rush upon your peace.

—————
198 *trumpet* trumpeter 201 *warned* summoned 205 *parle* conference
207 *advancèd* raised 208 *prospect* view 209 *endamagement* injury 215
winking closed as in sleep 216 *but* except 217 *waist* belt; *doth* do 218
compulsion . . . ordinance force of the guns' artillery 219 *lime* the cement
that holds stone walls together 220 *dishabited* dislodged

But on the sight of us your lawful king,
223 Who painfully with much expedient march
224 Have brought a countercheck before your gates,
To save unscratched your city's threatened cheeks,
226 Behold, the French amazed vouchsafe a parle;
And now, instead of bullets wrapped in fire,
To make a shaking fever in your walls,
229 They shoot but calm words folded up in smoke,
230 To make a faithless error in your ears.
Which trust accordingly, kind citizens,
232 And let us in, your king, whose labored spirits,
233 Forwearied in this action of swift speed,
234 Craves harborage within your city walls.

KING PHILIP
When I have said, make answer to us both.
236 Lo! In this right hand, whose protection
Is most divinely vowed upon the right
Of him it holds, stands young Plantagenet,
Son to the elder brother of this man,
240 And king o'er him and all that he enjoys.
241 For this downtrodden equity we tread
242 In warlike march these greens before your town,
Being no further enemy to you
244 Than the constraint of hospitable zeal,
In the relief of this oppressèd child,
Religiously provokes. Be pleasèd then
To pay that duty which you truly owe
248 To him that owes it, namely this young prince;

---

223 *painfully* laboriously; *expedient* speedy   224 *countercheck* (a rebuke – to the French)   226 *vouchsafe a parle* grant a discussion   229 *folded . . . smoke* cloaked in deceitfully obscure phrases   230 *faithless* perfidious, disloyal; *error* falsehood   232 *labored* oppressed by labor   233 *Forwearied* tired out; *action* campaign   234 *harborage* shelter, acceptance   236–38 *In . . . holds* in, or led by, my right hand, with which I have vowed to protect Arthur's right, whose hand it holds   240 *enjoys* possesses   241 *equity* right, principle   242 *greens* grassy ground outside the city gates   244 *constraint . . . zeal* requirement of hospitable exertion   248 *owes* owns

And then our arms, like to a muzzled bear,
Save in aspect, hath all offense sealed up.   250
Our cannons' malice vainly shall be spent   251
Against th' invulnerable clouds of heaven,
And with a blessèd and unvexed retire,   253
With unhacked swords and helmets all unbruised,
We will bear home that lusty blood again   255
Which here we came to spout against your town,
And leave your children, wives, and you, in peace.
But if you fondly pass our proffered offer,   258
'Tis not the roundure of your old-faced walls   259
Can hide you from our messengers of war,   260
Though all these English and their discipline   261
Were harbored in their rude circumference.
Then tell us, shall your city call us lord,
In that behalf which we have challenged it?   264
Or shall we give the signal to our rage
And stalk in blood to our possession?

CITIZEN
In brief, we are the King of England's subjects.
For him, and in his right, we hold this town.

KING JOHN
Acknowledge then the king, and let me in.

CITIZEN
That can we not; but he that proves the king,   270
To him will we prove loyal. Till that time
Have we rammed up our gates against the world.

KING JOHN
Doth not the crown of England prove the king?
And if not that, I bring you witnesses,
Twice fifteen thousand hearts of England's breed –

---

250 *Save in aspect* except for appearance; *sealed up* ended   **251** *vainly* fruit-
lessly   **253** *retire* withdrawal   **255** *lusty blood* fierce energy   **258** *fondly pass*
foolishly ignore   **259** *roundure* circumference   **260** *messengers of war* can-
nonballs   **261** *discipline* military skill   **264** *which* in which   **270** *proves* is
proved

BASTARD

276   Bastards, and else.

KING JOHN

     To verify our title with their lives.

KING PHILIP

278   As many and as well-born bloods as those –

BASTARD

     Some bastards, too.

KING PHILIP

280   Stand in his face to contradict his claim.

CITIZEN

281   Till you compound whose right is worthiest,
     We for the worthiest hold the right from both.

KING JOHN

     Then God forgive the sins of all those souls

284   That to their everlasting residence,

285   Before the dew of evening fall, shall fleet,
     In dreadful trial of our kingdom's king!

KING PHILIP

     Amen, amen! Mount, chevaliers! To arms!

BASTARD

288   Saint George, that swinged the dragon, and e'er since

289   Sits on's horseback at mine hostess' door,

290   Teach us some fence! *[To Austria]* Sirrah, were I at
     home

291   At your den, sirrah, with your lioness,

292   I would set an oxhead to your lion's hide,
     And make a monster of you.

AUSTRIA   Peace! No more.

---

276 *and else* and otherwise   278 *bloods* men of mettle, and of good family
280 *in his face* opposing him   281 *compound* agree   284 *everlasting residence* i.e., final resting place   285 *fleet* pass away   288 *swinged* thrashed
289 *mine hostess' door* i.e., the door of a tavern or inn, with a sign of Saint
George hanging above; *hostess* could also refer to a whore, who is "ridden"
sexually   290 *fence* swordsmanship, defense   291 *lioness* (a slang expression
for whore)   292–93 *set . . . you* cause you to grow the horns of a cuckold (a
common joke of the time)

BASTARD
　O tremble, for you hear the lion roar.
KING JOHN
　Up higher to the plain, where we'll set forth
　In best appointment all our regiments.   296
BASTARD
　Speed then, to take advantage of the field.   297
KING PHILIP
　It shall be so; and at the other hill
　Command the rest to stand. God, and our right! *Exeunt.*
　　　Here after excursions, enter the Herald of France with
　　　Trumpets, to the gates.
FRENCH HERALD
　You men of Angiers, open wide your gates,   300
　And let young Arthur, Duke of Britain, in,
　Who by the hand of France this day hath made
　Much work for tears in many an English mother,
　Whose sons lie scattered on the bleeding ground.
　Many a widow's husband groveling lies,   305
　Coldly embracing the discolored earth,
　And victory with little loss doth play
　Upon the dancing banners of the French,
　Who are at hand, triumphantly displayed,   309
　To enter conquerors and to proclaim   310
　Arthur of Bretagne England's king and yours.
　　　Enter English Herald, with Trumpet.
ENGLISH HERALD
　Rejoice, you men of Angiers, ring your bells.
　King John, your king and England's, doth approach,
　Commander of this hot malicious day.   314
　Their armors, that marched hence so silver-bright,
　Hither return all gilt with Frenchmen's blood.   316

---

296 *In best appointment* (1) in the most orderly (and efficacious) manner, (2)
with the best equipment   **297** *advantage* (1) strategic position (a "vantage"
point), (2) opportunity **305** *groveling* prone, on his belly **309** *displayed*
deployed, spread out **314** *hot malicious* hotly and violently fought **316**
gilt (1) made red, (2) ornamented, or gilded, as with gold

317   There stuck no plume in any English crest
318   That is removèd by a staff of France.
       Our colors do return in those same hands
320   That did display them when we first marched forth,
       And like a jolly troop of huntsmen come
322   Our lusty English, all with purpled hands
323   Dyed in the dying slaughter of their foes.
       Open your gates and give the victors way.

HUBERT
       Heralds, from off our towers we might behold,
326   From first to last, the onset and retire
       Of both your armies, whose equality
328   By our best eyes cannot be censurèd.
       Blood hath bought blood, and blows have answered
         blows,
330   Strength matched with strength, and power confronted
         power.
       Both are alike, and both alike we like.
       One must prove greatest. While they weigh so even,
       We hold our town for neither, yet for both.
           Enter the two Kings, with their powers, at several doors.

KING JOHN
       France, hast thou yet more blood to cast away?
335   Say, shall the current of our right run on?
       Whose passage, vexed with thy impediment,
337   Shall leave his native channel and o'erswell
       With course disturbed even thy confining shores,
       Unless thou let his silver water keep
340   A peaceful progress to the ocean.

KING PHILIP
       England, thou hast not saved one drop of blood

---

317 *crest* helmet 318 *staff* shaft of a spear 322 *purpled* bloody 323
Dyed . . . foes (it was a custom for hunters to dip their hands in the blood of
the slain deer) 326 *retire* retreat 328 *censurèd* estimated 335 *run* flow
337 *native channel* i.e., English boundaries 340 *progress* journey

In this hot trial more than we of France;
Rather, lost more. And by this hand I swear,
That sways the earth this climate overlooks,   344
Before we will lay down our just-borne arms,   345
We'll put thee down, 'gainst whom these arms we bear,   346
Or add a royal number to the dead,   347
Gracing the scroll that tells of this war's loss
With slaughter couplèd to the name of kings.

BASTARD
Ha, majesty! How high thy glory towers   350
When the rich blood of kings is set on fire!
O now doth death line his dread chaps with steel!   352
The swords of soldiers are his teeth, his fangs;
And now he feasts, mousing the flesh of men   354
In undetermined differences of kings.   355
Why stand these royal fronts amazèd thus?   356
Cry "havoc!", kings; back to the stainèd field,   357
You equal potents, fiery kindled spirits!   358
Then let confusion of one part confirm   359
The other's peace; till then, blows, blood, and death!   360

KING JOHN
Whose party do the townsmen yet admit?   361

KING PHILIP
Speak, citizens, for England; who's your king?

HUBERT
The King of England, when we know the king.

KING PHILIP
Know him in us, that here hold up his right.

---

344 *That ... overlooks* that rules the region under this portion – *climate* – of
the sky   345 *just-borne* (1) rightfully carried, (2) recently taken up   346 *put
thee down* (1) crush, (2) make a note of   347 *royal number* a royal item on
the scroll bearing the official list of the dead   352 *chaps* jaws   354 *mousing*
tearing   355 *undetermined differences* unsettled quarrels   356 *fronts* faces
(literally, foreheads)   357 *havoc* (this cry was a traditional signal for indis-
criminate slaughter with no taking of prisoners)   358 *potents* powers   359
confusion defeat; *part* party   361 *yet* now

KING JOHN

365 In us, that are our own great deputy,
And bear possession of our person here,
Lord of our presence, Angiers, and of you.

HUBERT

A greater power than we denies all this,
And till it be undoubted, we do lock
370 Our former scruple in our strong-barred gates,
371 Kinged of our fear, until our fears, resolved,
372 Be by some certain king purged and deposed.

BASTARD

373 By heaven, these scroyles of Angiers flout you, kings,
And stand securely on their battlements
As in a theater, whence they gape and point
At your industrious scenes and acts of death.
Your royal presences be ruled by me.
378 Do like the mutines of Jerusalem,
379 Be friends awhile and both conjointly bend
380 Your sharpest deeds of malice on this town.
381 By east and west let France and England mount
382 Their battering cannon chargèd to the mouths,
383 Till their soul-fearing clamors have brawled down
The flinty ribs of this contemptuous city.
385 I'd play incessantly upon these jades,
386 Even till unfencèd desolation
387 Leave them as naked as the vulgar air.
That done, dissever your united strengths,
And part your mingled colors once again;

---

365 *that ... deputy* i.e., who stand for my own right (King John uses the royal plural pronoun)   370 *former scruple* previous (and continuing) hesitation or concern   371 *Kinged of* ruled by   372 *Be* should be   373 *scroyles* scoundrels   378 *mutines of Jerusalem* (when Jerusalem was besieged by the emperor Titus, warring factions within the city united in common struggle against the Romans)   379 *bend* direct   381 *mount* aim   382 *chargèd ... mouths* fully loaded   383 *brawled down* beaten down with noise   385 *play ... jades* fire repeatedly upon these wretches (jades are decrepit horses)   386 *unfencèd* defenseless, unbounded   387 *naked* unarmed; *vulgar* common to all

Turn face to face and bloody point to point. 390
Then in a moment Fortune shall cull forth 391
Out of one side her happy minion, 392
To whom in favor she shall give the day,
And kiss him with a glorious victory.
How like you this wild counsel, mighty states? 395
Smacks it not something of the policy? 396

KING JOHN
Now, by the sky that hangs above our heads,
I like it well. France, shall we knit our powers
And lay this Angiers even with the ground,
Then after fight who shall be king of it? 400

BASTARD
And if thou hast the mettle of a king,
Being wronged as we are by this peevish town, 402
Turn thou the mouth of thy artillery,
As we will ours, against these saucy walls; 404
And when that we have dashed them to the ground,
Why then defy each other, and pell-mell 406
Make work upon ourselves, for heaven or hell. 407

KING PHILIP
Let it be so. Say, where will you assault?

KING JOHN
We from the west will send destruction
Into this city's bosom. 410

AUSTRIA
I from the north. 411

KING PHILIP   Our thunder from the south
Shall rain their drift of bullets on this town. 412

---

390 *point to point* weapon (e.g., sword) point to weapon point   **391** *Fortune* chance (commonly personified in medieval and Renaissance literature as a fickle goddess)   **392** *minion* sweetheart, favorite   **395** *states* kings   **396** *Smacks* rings, tastes; *it* i.e., the Bastard's idea; *policy* art of politics (in pejorative sense, involving trickery and deceit; the Bastard is rather naively boasting of his ability as a politician)   **402** *peevish* obstinate   **404** *saucy* impudent   **406** *pell-mell* in confusion   **407** *Make work* wage war   **410** *bosom* i.e., heart, center   **411** *thunder* cannon   **412** *drift* rain

BASTARD   *[Aside]*

413   O prudent discipline! From north to south
      Austria and France shoot in each other's mouth.

415   I'll stir them to it. Come, away, away!

HUBERT

416   Hear us, great kings; vouchsafe a while to stay,
      And I shall show you peace and fair-faced league,
      Win you this city without stroke or wound,
      Rescue those breathing lives to die in beds,

420   That here come sacrifices for the field.
      Persever not, but hear me, mighty kings.

KING JOHN

422   Speak on with favor; we are bent to hear.

HUBERT

      That daughter there of Spain, the Lady Blanche,

424   Is near to England. Look upon the years
      Of Lewis the Dauphin and that lovely maid.
      If lusty love should go in quest of beauty,
      Where should he find it fairer than in Blanche?

428   If zealous love should go in search of virtue,
      Where should he find it purer than in Blanche?

430   If love ambitious sought a match of birth,

431   Whose veins bound richer blood than Lady Blanche?
      Such as she is, in beauty, virtue, birth,

433   Is the young dauphin every way complete.

434   If not complete of, say he is not she,
      And she again wants nothing, to name want,
      If want it be not that she is not he.
      He is the half part of a blessèd man,

438   Left to be finishèd by such as she,

---

413 *discipline* military skill   415 *away, away* to it   416 *vouchsafe* please
422 *favor* permission; *bent* inclined   424 *near to England* a close relative of
King John   428 *zealous love* holy love, as opposed to lust   431 *bound* contain   433 *complete* perfect   434–36 *If . . . not he* (a type of wordplay in
which Elizabethans delighted, the sense being that each requires the other to
make his own perfection even more perfect)   438 *finishèd* completed, perfected

And she a fair divided excellence,   439
Whose fullness of perfection lies in him.   440
O, two such silver currents when they join   441
Do glorify the banks that bound them in;   442
And two such shores to two such streams made one,
Two such controlling bounds shall you be, kings,
To these two princes, if you marry them.
This union shall do more than battery can   446
To our fast-closèd gates; for at this match,   447
With swifter spleen than powder can enforce,   448
The mouth of passage shall we fling wide ope,   449
And give you entrance; but without this match,   450
The sea enragèd is not half so deaf,
Lions more confident, mountains and rocks
More free from motion, no, not Death himself
In mortal fury half so peremptory,   454
As we to keep this city.   455
BASTARD   Here's a stay,
That shakes the rotten carcase of old Death
Out of his rags! Here's a large mouth, indeed,   457
That spits forth death and mountains, rocks and seas,
Talks as familiarly of roaring lions
As maids of thirteen do of puppy dogs.   460
What cannoneer begot this lusty blood?
He speaks plain cannon fire and smoke and bounce.   462
He gives the bastinado with his tongue.   463
Our ears are cudgeled; not a word of his
But buffets better than a fist of France.
'Zounds! I was never so bethumped with words   466

---

439 *divided* partial, incomplete   **441** *silver currents* (marriage was often celebrated in Elizabethan love poetry as a joining of two streams of water)   **442** *bound them in* confine them   **446** *battery* force   **447** *match* (1) marriage, (2) the match that fires the cannon   **448** *spleen* violent energy; *powder* gunpowder (an anachronism)   **449** *mouth of passage* gate   **454** *peremptory* determined   **455** *stay* obstacle   **457** *rags* (death was often portrayed in medieval art as a skeleton clad in rags)   **462** *bounce* bang   **463** *bastinado* a beating with a stick   **466** *'Zounds* by God's wounds

Since I first called my brother's father dad.

ELEANOR

468 Son, list to this conjunction, make this match.
Give with our niece a dowry large enough,
470 For by this knot thou shalt so surely tie
471 Thy now unsured assurance to the crown
472 That yon green boy shall have no sun to ripe
The bloom that promiseth a mighty fruit.
I see a yielding in the looks of France.
475 Mark how they whisper. Urge them while their souls
476 Are capable of this ambition,
477 Lest zeal, now melted by the windy breath
478 Of soft petitions, pity, and remorse,
Cool and congeal again to what it was.

HUBERT

480 Why answer not the double majesties
481 This friendly treaty of our threatened town?

KING PHILIP

482 Speak England first, that hath been forward first
To speak unto this city. What say you?

KING JOHN

If that the dauphin there, thy princely son,
Can in this book of beauty read "I love,"
Her dowry shall weigh equal with a queen;
487 For Angiers and fair Touraine, Maine, Poitiers,
488 And all that we upon this side the sea,
Except this city now by us besieged,
490 Find liable to our crown and dignity,
Shall gild her bridal bed and make her rich
492 In titles, honors, and promotions,

---

468 *list* listen   470 *knot* i.e., marriage contract   471 *unsured* insecure   472 *green* i.e., young   475 *Mark* note   476 *capable of* susceptible to; *ambition* desire to come to terms   477–79 *Lest . . . what it was* lest the French king's desire to help Arthur, now melted by the pleas of the citizens of Angiers, become as firm as it was before   478 *remorse* compassion   481 *treaty* proposal   482 *forward* eager   487 *Angiers* i.e., Anjou   488 *the* of the   490 *liable* subject   492 *promotions* elevations in rank

As she in beauty, education, blood,
Holds hand with any princess of the world.   494

KING PHILIP
What sayst thou, boy? Look in the lady's face.

LEWIS
I do, my lord, and in her eye I find
A wonder or a wondrous miracle,
The shadow of myself formed in her eye,   498
Which, being but the shadow of your son,   499
Becomes a sun, and makes your son a shadow.   500
I do protest I never loved myself
Till now infixèd I beheld myself,   502
Drawn in the flattering table of her eye.   503
    Whispers with Blanche.

BASTARD
Drawn in the flattering table of her eye!   504
Hanged in the frowning wrinkle of her brow!
And quartered in her heart! He doth espy   506
Himself love's traitor; this is pity now,   507
That hanged and drawn and quartered, there should be
In such a love so vile a lout as he.

BLANCHE
My uncle's will in this respect is mine.   510
If he see aught in you that makes him like,   511
That anything he sees which moves his liking,
I can with ease translate it to my will;   513
Or if you will, to speak more properly,
I will enforce it easily to my love.

---

494 *Holds hand with* equals 498 *shadow* reflection 499 *son* (with pun on
sun) 502 *infixèd* fastened, inscribed 503 *Drawn* pictured; *table* flat surface on which a picture is painted 504 *table* drawing tablet 504–6 (the
Bastard quibbles here on the punishment for treason: hanging, drawing [dis-
emboweling], and quartering [cutting the traitor's body into four parts];
quartered can also connote "housed," "lodged") 506 *espy* spy 507 *love's
traitor* a traitor in love; *is* is a 510 *will* intention (but perhaps also sexual desire) 511 *aught* anything 513 *translate it to my will* cause it to suit my own
desires

Further I will not flatter you, my lord,
That all I see in you is worthy love,
Than this: that nothing do I see in you,
519 Though churlish thoughts themselves should be your
       judge,
520 That I can find should merit any hate.

KING JOHN
What say these young ones? What say you, my niece?

BLANCHE
522 That she is bound in honor still to do
What you in wisdom still vouchsafe to say.

KING JOHN
Speak then, Prince Dauphin. Can you love this lady?

LEWIS
Nay, ask me if I can refrain from love,
For I do love her most unfeignèdly.

KING JOHN
Then do I give Volquessen, Touraine, Maine,
Poitiers, and Anjou, these five provinces,
529 With her to thee; and this addition more,
530 Full thirty thousand marks of English coin.
Philip of France, if thou be pleased withal,
Command thy son and daughter to join hands.

KING PHILIP
533 It likes us well. Young princes, close your hands.

AUSTRIA
And your lips too, for I am well assured
535 That I did so when I was first assured.

KING PHILIP
Now, citizens of Angiers, ope your gates,
537 Let in that amity which you have made,
538 For at Saint Mary's chapel presently

---

519 *churlish* miserly (of praise) 522, 523 *still* always 529 *addition* extra
provision 530 *Full* fully; *marks* coins worth two thirds of a pound 533
likes pleases; *close . . . hands* take each other's hand 535 *assured* engaged
537 *amity* league 538 *presently* immediately

The rites of marriage shall be solemnized.
Is not the Lady Constance in this troop?   540
I know she is not, for this match made up   541
Her presence would have interrupted much.
Where is she and her son? Tell me, who knows.

LEWIS
    She is sad and passionate at your highness' tent.   544

KING PHILIP
    And, by my faith, this league that we have made
    Will give her sadness very little cure.
    Brother of England, how may we content
    This widow lady? In her right we came,   548
    Which we, God knows, have turned another way,
    To our own vantage.   550

KING JOHN   We will heal up all,
    For we'll create young Arthur Duke of Bretagne   551
    And Earl of Richmond, and this rich fair town
    We make him lord of. Call the Lady Constance.
    Some speedy messenger bid her repair
    To our solemnity. I trust we shall,   555
    If not fill up the measure of her will,   556
    Yet in some measure satisfy her so,   557
    That we shall stop her exclamation.   558
    Go we, as well as haste will suffer us,   559
    To this unlooked for, unprepar̀d pomp.   560
                    Exeunt [all but the Bastard].

BASTARD
    Mad world! Mad kings! Mad composition!   561
    John, to stop Arthur's title in the whole,
    Hath willingly departed with a part,   563

---

541 *made up* having been agreed   544 *passionate* angry   548 *right* cause, behalf   550 *vantage* advantage, profit   551 *Bretagne* northwest region of
France   555 *our solemnity* the wedding ceremony   556 *measure* measuring
cup; *will* desire   557 *in some measure* in some respect, to some degree   558
stop her exclamation silence her loud complaints   559 *suffer* permit   561
composition agreement   563 *departed with* relinquished

564 And France, whose armor conscience buckled on,
Whom zeal and charity brought to the field
566 As God's own soldier, rounded in the ear
567 With that same purpose-changer, that sly devil,
568 That broker, that still breaks the pate of faith,
That daily break-vow, he that wins of all,
570 Of kings, of beggars, old men, young men, maids,
571 Who, having no external thing to lose
But the word "maid," cheats the poor maid of that,
573 That smooth-faced gentleman, tickling commodity,
574 Commodity, the bias of the world;
575 The world, who of itself is peisèd well,
576 Made to run even upon even ground,
577 Till this advantage, this vile-drawing bias,
578 This sway of motion, this commodity,
579 Makes it take head from all indifferency,
580 From all direction, purpose, course, intent.
And this same bias, this commodity,
582 This bawd, this broker, this all-changing word,
583 Clapped on the outward eye of fickle France,
584 Hath drawn him from his own determined aid,
585 From a resolved and honorable war,
To a most base and vile-concluded peace.
587 And why rail I on this commodity?
588 But for because he hath not wooed me yet.
589 Not that I have the power to clutch my hand

---

564 *conscience* true belief (as opposed to mere territorialism)   566 *rounded* whispered   567 *With* by   568 *broker* go-between (in a pejorative sense, as a pander)   571 *Who* i.e., the maids   573 *smooth-faced* clean-shaven (and thus smooth-talking); *tickling* flattering; *commodity* self-interest   574 *bias* the weight in a bowling ball that causes it to curve   575 *peisèd* balanced, weighted   576 *even* evenly; *even* level   577 *vile-drawing* leading into evil   578 *motion* movement, momentum   579 *take . . . indifferency* rush away from all moderation   582 *bawd* pander, pimp   583 *outward eye* (1) ocular (as opposed to internal, moral) vision, (2) *eye* = hole in the bowling ball that held the lead weight; *France* Philip   584 *determined* decided upon   585 *resolved* already decided upon   587 *rail . . . on* abuse, slander   588 *But for because* merely because   589 *clutch* close (and thus decline to accept)

When his fair angels would salute my palm,   590
But for my hand, as unattempted yet,   591
Like a poor beggar, raileth on the rich.
Well, whiles I am a beggar, I will rail   593
And say there is no sin but to be rich;
And being rich, my virtue then shall be   595
To say there is no vice but beggary.   596
Since kings break faith upon commodity,   597
Gain, be my lord, for I will worship thee!   *Exit.*

*

∾ **III.1** *Enter Constance, Arthur, and Salisbury.*

CONSTANCE
Gone to be married! Gone to swear a peace!
False blood to false blood joined! Gone to be friends!   2
Shall Lewis have Blanche, and Blanche those provinces?
It is not so; thou hast misspoke, misheard.
Be well advised, tell o'er thy tale again.
It cannot be; thou dost but say 'tis so.
I trust I may not trust thee, for thy word
Is but the vain breath of a common man.   8
Believe me, I do not believe thee, man;
I have a king's oath to the contrary.   10
Thou shalt be punished for thus frighting me,
For I am sick and capable of fears,   12
Oppressed with wrongs, and therefore full of fears,
A widow, husbandless, subject to fears,
A woman, naturally born to fears;   15

---

590 *angels* Elizabethan gold coins bearing the relief of an angel, worth slightly more than half a pound sterling; *salute* greet   591 *unattempted* untempted   593 *whiles* while   595 *virtue* (1) habit, (2) moral code   596 *beggary* poverty   597 *faith* promises; *upon* because of
   III.1 The French camp   2 *False* faithless   8 *common* not that of a king   12 *capable of* susceptible to   15 *naturally born to* by nature heir to (women were thought to be timid)

16   And though thou now confess thou didst but jest,
17   With my vexed spirits I cannot take a truce,
     But they will quake and tremble all this day.
     What dost thou mean by shaking of thy head?
20   Why dost thou look so sadly on my son?
     What means that hand upon that breast of thine?
22   Why holds thine eye that lamentable rheum,
23   Like a proud river peering o'er his bounds?
     Be these sad signs confirmers of thy words?
     Then speak again, not all thy former tale,
     But this one word, whether thy tale be true.

SALISBURY

27   As true as I believe you think them false
28   That give you cause to prove my saying true.

CONSTANCE

     O if thou teach me to believe this sorrow,
30   Teach thou this sorrow how to make me die!
31   And let belief and life encounter so
     As doth the fury of two desperate men
     Which in the very meeting fall and die.
34   Lewis marry Blanche! O boy, then where art thou?
     France friend with England, what becomes of me?
36   Fellow, be gone! I cannot brook thy sight.
     This news hath made thee a most ugly man.

SALISBURY

     What other harm have I, good lady, done,
     But spoke the harm that is by others done?

CONSTANCE

40   Which harm within itself so heinous is
     As it makes harmful all that speak of it.

---

16 *though* if   17 *take a truce* make peace   20 *sadly* sorrowfully, solemnly
22 *rheum* moisture, tears   23 *peering o'er* overflowing   27 *them* i.e., the
French king and his advisers   28 *cause* reason, warrant   31 *encounter* meet
in combat   34 *boy* i.e., Arthur; *where art thou* what will become of your
claims   36 *brook* stand, tolerate

ARTHUR
  I do beseech you, madam, be content.   42
CONSTANCE
  If thou that bid'st me be content wert grim,
  Ugly and slanderous to thy mother's womb,   44
  Full of unpleasing blots and sightless stains,   45
  Lame, foolish, crooked, swart, prodigious,   46
  Patched with foul moles and eye-offending marks,   47
  I would not care, I then would be content,
  For then I should not love thee; no, nor thou
  Become thy great birth, nor deserve a crown.   50
  But thou art fair, and at thy birth, dear boy,
  Nature and Fortune joined to make thee great.
  Of nature's gifts thou mayst with lilies boast   53
  And with the half-blown rose. But Fortune, O!   54
  She is corrupted, changed, and won from thee.
  Sh' adulterates hourly with thine uncle John,   56
  And with her golden hand hath plucked on France   57
  To tread down fair respect of sovereignty,   58
  And made his majesty the bawd to theirs.
  France is a bawd to Fortune and King John,   60
  That strumpet Fortune, that usurping John!   61
  Tell me, thou fellow, is not France forsworn?   62
  Envenom him with words, or get thee gone   63
  And leave those woes alone which I alone
  Am bound to underbear.   65
SALISBURY   Pardon me, madam,

---

42 *content* calm, quiet   44 *slanderous* a disgrace   45 *blots* blemishes; *sightless*
unsightly   46 *swart* of dark complexion (and hence morally unworthy, according to Elizabethan theories); *prodigious* monstrous   47 *foul moles* (moles
were considered blemishes and a sign of moral faults)   50 *Become* be worthy
of   53 *lilies* i.e., (1) a pure white flower, (2) the French royal insignia   54
half-blown half-blossomed (and thus innocent)   56 *adulterates* (1) commits
adultery, (2) changes, shows her fickleness; *hourly* frequently   57 *with her*
golden hand by bribery; *plucked on* incited   58 *fair respect of* proper regard
for   61 *strumpet* hussy, whore   62 *forsworn* in violation of his promise   63
Envenom vituperate   65 *underbear* endure

I may not go without you to the kings.

CONSTANCE
Thou mayst, thou shalt; I will not go with thee.
I will instruct my sorrows to be proud,
69   For grief is proud and makes his owner stoop.
70   To me and to the state of my great grief
Let kings assemble, for my grief's so great
That no supporter but the huge firm earth
Can hold it up. Here I and sorrows sit.
Here is my throne; bid kings come bow to it.
      Enter King John, [King Philip of] France, [Lewis the]
      Dauphin, Blanche, Eleanor, Philip [the Bastard],
      Austria [, and Attendants].

KING PHILIP
'Tis true, fair daughter, and this blessèd day
76   Ever in France shall be kept festival.
77   To solemnize this day the glorious sun
78   Stays in his course and plays the alchemist,
Turning with splendor of his precious eye
80   The meager cloddy earth to glittering gold.
The yearly course that brings this day about
Shall never see it but a holy day.

CONSTANCE
A wicked day, and not a holy day!
What hath this day deserved? What hath it done
85   That it in golden letters should be set
86   Among the high tides in the calendar?
87   Nay, rather turn this day out of the week,
This day of shame, oppression, perjury.

---

69 *grief . . . stoop* (Constance sees herself as the slave of the grief that she possesses but that masters her)   **70** *state* royal court   **76** *festival* as a holiday   **77** *solemnize* (1) commemorate, (2) bless   **78** *Stays* pauses; *course* path through the sky; *alchemist* person who attempts to turn base metals into gold   **80** *meager* barren   **85** *in golden letters* i.e., marked off in different type (or manuscript) and color (as was the practice in both Elizabethan printing practice and medieval manuscripts)   **86** *high tides* great festivals   **87** *turn . . . out* excise this day from the calendar

Or, if it must stand still, let wives with child   89
Pray that their burdens may not fall this day,   90
Lest that their hopes prodigiously be crossed.   91
But on this day let seamen fear no wrack;   92
No bargains break that are not this day made;
This day all things begun come to ill end;
Yea, faith itself to hollow falsehood change!

KING PHILIP
By heaven, lady, you shall have no cause
To curse the fair proceedings of this day.
Have I not pawned to you my majesty?   98

CONSTANCE
You have beguiled me with a counterfeit   99
Resembling majesty, which, being touched and tried,   100
Proves valueless. You are forsworn, forsworn.
You came in arms to spill mine enemies' blood,   102
But now in arms you strengthen it with yours.   103
The grappling vigor and rough frown of war
Is cold in amity and painted peace,   105
And our oppression hath made up this league.   106
Arm, arm, you heavens, against these perjured kings!
A widow cries; be husband to me, heavens!   108
Let not the hours of this ungodly day
Wear out the day in peace; but, ere sunset,   110
Set armèd discord 'twixt these perjured kings!
Hear me! O, hear me!   112

AUSTRIA   Lady Constance, peace!

CONSTANCE
War! War! No peace! Peace is to me a war.

---

89 *stand still* remain; *with child* pregnant   91 *prodigiously be crossed* be disappointed by the birth of a monster   92 *But* except; *wrack* shipwreck   98 *pawned* pledged   99 *counterfeit* false coin   100 *touched and tried* tested by being rubbed on a touchstone   102 *in arms* wearing armor   103 *in arms* embracing one another; *yours* your blood relative, Lewis   105 *Is . . . peace* lies dead in a new friendship and pretended peace   106 *oppression* distress; *league* truce, union   108 *be husband* i.e., defend my cause as a husband would   112 *peace* be quiet, calm

114 O, Limoges! O, Austria! Thou dost shame
115 That bloody spoil. Thou slave, thou wretch, thou cow-
         ard!
         Thou little valiant, great in villainy!
         Thou ever strong upon the stronger side!
118 Thou Fortune's champion, that dost never fight
119 But when her humorous ladyship is by
120 To teach thee safety! Thou art perjured too,
121 And sooth'st up greatness. What a fool art thou,
122 A ramping fool, to brag and stamp and swear
123 Upon my party! Thou cold-blooded slave,
         Hast thou not spoke like thunder on my side,
         Been sworn my soldier, bidding me depend
         Upon thy stars, thy fortune, and thy strength,
127 And dost thou now fall over to my foes?
128 Thou wear a lion's hide! Doff it for shame,
129 And hang a calfskin on those recreant limbs.

AUSTRIA
130 O that a man should speak those words to me!

BASTARD
         And hang a calfskin on those recreant limbs.

AUSTRIA
132 Thou dar'st not say so, villain, for thy life.

BASTARD
         And hang a calfskin on those recreant limbs.

KING JOHN
134 We like not this; thou dost forget thyself.
         Enter Pandulph.

---

114 *Limoges* i.e., Austria (Shakespeare conflates the historical Duke Leopold
of Austria and Viscount Vidomar of Limoges, at whose castle Richard I received his death wound)   115 *bloody spoil* i.e., the lion skin he wears   118
Fortune's champion knight who fights in Fortune's cause   119 *humorous*
fickle, capricious   121 *sooth'st up* flatter   122 *ramping* rushing wildly about
like a lion   123 *Upon my party* to my side   127 *fall over* desert   128 *Doff*
remove   129 *calfskin* (material of which coats for household fools traditionally were made; alluding also to the cowardice of Austria); *recreant* cowardly
130 *that* if only   132 *villain* i.e., base person   134 *thou* i.e., the Bastard;
forget thyself i.e., forget your place and conduct proper to it

KING PHILIP

Here comes the holy legate of the pope.   135

PANDULPH

Hail, you anointed deputies of God!   136
To thee, King John, my holy errand is.
I Pandulph, of fair Milan cardinal,
And from Pope Innocent the legate here,
Do in his name religiously demand   140
Why thou against the church, our holy mother,
So willfully dost spurn; and force perforce   142
Keep Stephen Langton, chosen Archbishop
Of Canterbury, from that holy see.   144
This, in our foresaid holy father's name,
Pope Innocent, I do demand of thee.

KING JOHN

What earthy name to interrogatories   147
Can test the free breath of a sacred king?
Thou canst not, cardinal, devise a name
So slight, unworthy and ridiculous,   150
To charge me to an answer, as the pope.   151
Tell him this tale, and from the mouth of England
Add thus much more, that no Italian priest   153
Shall tithe or toll in our dominions,   154
But as we under God are supreme head,   155
So under him that great supremacy,
Where we do reign, we will alone uphold,
Without th' assistance of a mortal hand.

---

135 *legate* ambassador, representative   136 *anointed deputies* (kings were
thought to be God's representatives on earth, and were anointed as such in
their coronations)   142 *spurn* oppose with contempt; *force perforce* by
forcible means   144 *from* from taking up his office as archbishop; *see* ecclesiastical jurisdiction   147–48 *What . . . king* what mortal man can compel a
king to answer questions   147 *interrogatories* formal questions put to a witness in a court of law   151 *charge* command   153 *Italian priest* (a term of
contempt for the pope – whom Elizabethans also referred to, in a similar
vein, as the "Bishop of Rome")   154 *tithe or toll* collect church revenues
155 *supreme head* leader of the church (a title not official until 1534, when it
was granted to Henry VIII by Parliament after his break with Rome)

159   So tell the pope, all reverence set apart
160   To him and his usurped authority.

KING PHILIP
    Brother of England, you blaspheme in this.

KING JOHN
    Though you and all the kings of Christendom
163   Are led so grossly by this meddling priest,
164   Dreading the curse that money may buy out,
    And by the merit of vile gold, dross, dust,
    Purchase corrupted pardon of a man,
167   Who in that sale sells pardon from himself,
    Though you and all the rest, so grossly led,
169   This juggling witchcraft with revenue cherish,
170   Yet I alone, alone do me oppose
    Against the pope, and count his friends my foes.

PANDULPH
    Then, by the lawful power that I have,
173   Thou shalt stand cursed and excommunicate;
    And blessèd shall he be that doth revolt
175   From his allegiance to an heretic;
    And meritorious shall that hand be called,
    Canonized and worshiped as a saint,
178   That takes away by any secret course
    Thy hateful life.

CONSTANCE   O lawful let it be
180   That I have room with Rome to curse awhile!
    Good father cardinal, cry thou amen

---

159 *set apart* discarded   **163** *grossly* stupidly   **164** *buy out* bribe, ransom (King John inveighs here against the Catholic practice of paying money to the church for one's sins – buying a "pardon" – as a way to absolve oneself from them)   **167** *from himself* (1) i.e., only from himself, and not from God, (2) damns himself in the practice of such sales   **169** *witchcraft* super-stition   **173** *excommunicate* excommunicated, exiled from the community of the church (a grave punishment for anyone, and especially dangerous for a king, whose subjects might consider themselves absolved of loyalty and oaths)   **175** *heretic* infidel, unbeliever   **178** *secret course* covert means (poison, for instance)   **180** *have room* can join

To my keen curses, for without my wrong   182
There is no tongue hath power to curse him right.

PANDULPH
There's law and warrant, lady, for my curse.

CONSTANCE
And for mine too. When law can do no right,
Let it be lawful that law bar no wrong.
Law cannot give my child his kingdom here,
For he that holds his kingdom holds the law;   188
Therefore, since law itself is perfect wrong,
How can the law forbid my tongue to curse?   190

PANDULPH
Philip of France, on peril of a curse,
Let go the hand of that arch-heretic,   192
And raise the power of France upon his head,   193
Unless he do submit himself to Rome.

ELEANOR
Look'st thou pale, France? Do not let go thy hand.

CONSTANCE
Look to that, devil, lest that France repent,   196
And by disjoining hands, hell lose a soul.

AUSTRIA
King Philip, listen to the cardinal.

BASTARD
And hang a calfskin on his recreant limbs.

AUSTRIA
Well, ruffian, I must pocket up these wrongs,   200
Because –

BASTARD   Your breeches best may carry them.

KING JOHN
Philip, what sayst thou to the cardinal?

182–83 *without . . . right* he cannot be adequately cursed without recogni-
tion of his wrong against me   188 *holds . . . holds the law* possesses Arthur's
kingdom also administers its laws   192 *Let go the hand* break your truce
(and perhaps literally release John's hand, which would require that Philip
take it up at some point, probably during Constance's speech)   193 *upon*
against   196 *devil* i.e., Eleanor   200 *pocket up* put up with

CONSTANCE

203　What should he say, but as the cardinal?

LEWIS

204　Bethink you, father, for the difference
　　Is purchase of a heavy curse from Rome,
　　Or the light loss of England for a friend.

207　Forgo the easier.

BLANCHE　　　　　That's the curse of Rome.

CONSTANCE

　　O Lewis, stand fast! The devil tempts thee here

209　In likeness of a new untrimmèd bride.

BLANCHE

210　The Lady Constance speaks not from her faith,
　　But from her need.

CONSTANCE　　　　O, if thou grant my need,
　　Which only lives but by the death of faith,

213　That need must needs infer this principle,
　　That faith would live again by death of need.

215　O then, tread down my need, and faith mounts up;
　　Keep my need up, and faith is trodden down!

KING JOHN

217　The king is moved and answers not to this.

CONSTANCE

　　O be removed from him, and answer well!

AUSTRIA

　　Do so, King Philip; hang no more in doubt.

BASTARD

220　Hang nothing but a calfskin, most sweet lout.

KING PHILIP

　　I am perplexed, and know not what to say.

PANDULPH

　　What canst thou say but will perplex thee more,

---

203 *as the cardinal* i.e., as the cardinal says　**204** *difference* the price, the consequence　**207** *Forgo the easier* relinquish the less important　**209** *In likeness* in the guise of; *untrimmèd* unadorned　**213** *needs* of necessity　**215** *tread down* trample on　**217** *moved* disturbed, angered

If thou stand excommunicate and cursed?
KING PHILIP
Good reverend father, make my person yours,   224
And tell me how you would bestow yourself.   225
This royal hand and mine are newly knit,
And the conjunction of our inward souls   227
Married in league, coupled and linked together
With all religious strength of sacred vows.
The latest breath that gave the sound of words   230
Was deep-sworn faith, peace, amity, true love
Between our kingdoms and our royal selves,
And even before this truce, but new before,   233
No longer than we well could wash our hands
To clap this royal bargain up of peace,   235
Heaven knows, they were besmeared and overstained   236
With slaughter's pencil, where revenge did paint
The fearful difference of incensèd kings.   238
And shall these hands, so lately purged of blood,
So newly joined in love, so strong in both,   *240*
Unyoke this seizure and this kind regreet?   241
Play fast and loose with faith? So jest with heaven,   242
Make such unconstant children of ourselves,   243
As now again to snatch our palm from palm,
Unswear faith sworn, and on the marriage bed
Of smiling peace to march a bloody host,   246
And make a riot on the gentle brow
Of true sincerity? O holy sir,
My reverend father, let it not be so!
Out of your grace, devise, ordain, impose   250

---

224 *make my person yours* put yourself in my position   225 *bestow yourself*
behave   227 *inward souls* consciences   230 *latest breath* most recent speech
233 *new before* immediately preceding   235 *clap* strike the hands together to
seal a bargain   236 *overstained* colored, tinted   238 *fearful* fearsome, fear-
inducing; *difference* quarrel   241 *Unyoke this seizure* separate the hands
clasped in friendship; *regreet* return of the salutation of friendship   242 *Play
fast and loose* cheat   243 *unconstant* fickle   246 *host* army   250 *Out . . .
grace* with the power of your office

251　Some gentle order, and then we shall be blessed
　　　To do your pleasure and continue friends.

PANDULPH
　　　All form is formless, order orderless,
254　Save what is opposite to England's love.
　　　Therefore to arms! Be champion of our church,
　　　Or let the church, our mother, breathe her curse,
　　　A mother's curse, on her revolting son.
　　　France, thou mayst hold a serpent by the tongue,
259　A casèd lion by the mortal paw,
260　A fasting tiger safer by the tooth,
　　　Than keep in peace that hand which thou dost hold.

KING PHILIP
262　I may disjoin my hand, but not my faith.

PANDULPH
263　So mak'st thou faith an enemy to faith,
　　　And like a civil war set'st oath to oath,
　　　Thy tongue against thy tongue. O, let thy vow
　　　First made to heaven, first be to heaven performed,
　　　That is, to be the champion of our church.
268　What since thou swor'st is sworn against thyself
　　　And may not be performèd by thyself,
270　For that which thou hast sworn to do amiss
　　　Is not amiss when it is truly done;
　　　And being not done, where doing tends to ill,
　　　The truth is then most done not doing it.
　　　The better act of purposes mistook
　　　Is to mistake again; though indirect,

---

251 *order* solution, compromise　254 *Save . . . opposite* except that which
goes against, rejects　259 *casèd* caged; *mortal* deadly　262 *faith* promise
263–65 *So . . . tongue* you are swearing against the religious faith to which
you already are pledged　268 *What . . . swor'st* whatever you have sworn
since swearing your faith to the church　270–78 *For . . . burned* i.e., Philip
by not performing what he has just vowed may turn his wrong to right;
when one has done wrong it is often easier to return to the true path by another wrong than to retrace one's steps (this doctrine of equivocation was
particularly hated by Elizabethan Protestants)

Yet indirection thereby grows direct,
And falsehood falsehood cures, as fire cools fire
Within the scorchèd veins of one new burned.
It is religion that doth make vows kept,
But thou hast sworn against religion,   280
By what thou swear'st, against the thing thou swear'st,
And mak'st an oath the surety for thy truth   282
Against an oath; the truth thou art unsure
To swear swears only not to be forsworn;
Else what a mockery should it be to swear!
But thou dost swear only to be forsworn;
And most forsworn to keep what thou dost swear.
Therefore thy later vows against thy first
Is in thyself rebellion to thyself,
And better conquest never canst thou make   *290*
Than arm thy constant and thy nobler parts   291
Against these giddy loose suggestions;   292
Upon which better part our prayers come in,   293
If thou vouchsafe them. But, if not, then know
The peril of our curses light on thee   295
So heavy as thou shalt not shake them off,   296
But in despair die under their black weight.   297

AUSTRIA
Rebellion, flat rebellion!   298

BASTARD   Will 't not be?
Will not a calfskin stop that mouth of thine?

LEWIS
Father, to arms!   *300*

BLANCHE   Upon thy wedding day?
Against the blood that thou hast marrièd?   301

280–87 *But . . . swear* since you have sworn by your faith against your faith
(true religion), you make a mockery of swearing; you commit the greatest
breach of faith by keeping the oath you have just sworn 282 *surety* pledge,
guarantee 291 *arm* by arming 292 *giddy* unsafe, insecure; *suggestions*
temptations 293 *Upon . . . part* on whose more deserving behalf 295 *light*
descend 296 *as* that 297 *black* dark, doom-laden 298 *Will 't not be* is
nothing of any use 301 *blood* blood relationship

302 What, shall our feast be kept with slaughtered men?
303 Shall braying trumpets and loud churlish drums,
304 Clamors of hell, be measures to our pomp?
O husband, hear me! Ay, alack, how new
Is "husband" in my mouth! Even for that name,
Which till this time my tongue did ne'er pronounce,
Upon my knee I beg, go not to arms
Against mine uncle.

CONSTANCE   O, upon my knee,
310 Made hard with kneeling, I do pray to thee,
311 Thou virtuous dauphin, alter not the doom
312 Forethought by heaven.

BLANCHE
Now shall I see thy love. What motive may
Be stronger with thee than the name of wife?

CONSTANCE
That which upholdeth him that thee upholds,
His honor. O thine honor, Lewis, thine honor!

LEWIS
I muse your majesty doth seem so cold,
318 When such profound respects do pull you on.

PANDULPH
319 I will denounce a curse upon his head.

KING PHILIP
320 Thou shalt not need. England, I will fall from thee.

CONSTANCE
O fair return of banished majesty!

ELEANOR
O foul revolt of French inconstancy!

KING JOHN
France, thou shalt rue this hour within this hour.

---

302 *kept* celebrated   303 *churlish* rude   304 *measures* melodies   311 *doom* decision   312 *Forethought* predestined   318 *profound respects* weighty considerations   319 *denounce* proclaim   320 *fall from* forsake

BASTARD

    Old time the clock setter, that bald sexton time,   324
    Is it as he will? Well then, France shall rue.

BLANCHE

    The sun's o'ercast with blood. Fair day, adieu!
    Which is the side that I must go withal?
    I am with both. Each army hath a hand,
    And in their rage, I having hold of both,
    They whirl asunder and dismember me.   330
    Husband, I cannot pray that thou mayst win.
    Uncle, I needs must pray that thou mayst lose.
    Father, I may not wish the fortune thine.   333
    Grandam, I will not wish thy wishes thrive.
    Whoever wins, on that side shall I lose;
    Assurèd loss before the match be played.

LEWIS

    Lady, with me, with me thy fortune lies.

BLANCHE

    There where my fortune lives, there my life dies.

KING JOHN

    Cousin, go draw our puissance together.   339

                      [Exit the Bastard.]
    France, I am burned up with inflaming wrath,   340
    A rage whose heat hath this condition,   341
    That nothing can allay, nothing but blood,
    The blood, and dearest-valued blood, of France.   343

KING PHILIP

    Thy rage shall burn thee up, and thou shalt turn
    To ashes, ere our blood shall quench that fire.
    Look to thyself, thou art in jeopardy.

---

324 *Old time the clock setter* (the sexton's job included setting the church clock as well as digging graves; he is thus easily identified with *time,* the destroyer of life)   **333** *Father* i.e., father-in-law   **339** *Cousin* kinsman; *draw our puissance* muster our army   **341** *condition* quality   **343** *dearest-valued* (1) royal, (2) most necessary to life

KING JOHN
347   No more than he that threats. To arms let's hie!

Exeunt.

*

❧ **III.2** *Alarums, excursions. Enter Bastard, with Austria's head.*

BASTARD
Now, by my life, this day grows wondrous hot.
2   Some airy devil hovers in the sky
And pours down mischief. Austria's head lie there,
4   While Philip breathes.
Enter [King] John, Arthur, Hubert.
KING JOHN
5   Hubert, keep this boy. Philip, make up;
6   My mother is assailèd in our tent,
7   And ta'en, I fear.
BASTARD   My lord, I rescued her;
Her highness is in safety, fear you not.
But on, my liege, for very little pains
10   Will bring this labor to a happy end.

Exit [with the others].

*

❧ **III.3** *Alarums, excursions, retreat. Enter [King] John, Eleanor, Arthur, Bastard, Hubert, Lords.*

KING JOHN   *[To Eleanor]*
So shall it be; your grace shall stay behind
So strongly guarded. *[To Arthur]* Cousin, look not sad.

---

347 *threats* threatens; *hie* hurry
    III.2 Near the English camp   2 *Some . . . sky* a thunderstorm threatens
4 *breathes* rests   5 *make up* advance to the front line   6 *assailèd* attacked
7 *ta'en* taken prisoner
    III.3 The English camp

Thy grandam loves thee, and thy uncle will
As dear be to thee as thy father was.

ARTHUR
O this will make my mother die with grief!

KING JOHN   *[To the Bastard]*
Cousin, away for England! Haste before,   6
And ere our coming see thou shake the bags   7
Of hoarding abbots; imprisoned angels   8
Set at liberty. The fat ribs of peace
Must by the hungry now be fed upon.   10
Use our commission in his utmost force.   11

BASTARD
Bell, book, and candle shall not drive me back   12
When gold and silver becks me to come on.   13
I leave your highness. Grandam, I will pray –
If ever I remember to be holy –
For your fair safety; so I kiss your hand.

ELEANOR
Farewell, gentle cousin.   17

KING JOHN   Coz, farewell.

                                   [Exit the Bastard.]

ELEANOR
Come hither, little kinsman. Hark, a word.
   [She takes Arthur aside.]

KING JOHN
Come hither, Hubert. O my gentle Hubert,
We owe thee much! Within this wall of flesh   20
There is a soul counts thee her creditor,   21
And with advantage means to pay thy love;   22
And, my good friend, thy voluntary oath   23
Lives in this bosom, dearly cherishèd.

---

6 *before* ahead of us   7 *bags* i.e., moneybags   8 *abbots* leaders of monasteries;
angels coins (with the usual pun)   11 *commission* delegated authority; *his* its
12 *Bell, book, and candle* instruments used in the ritual of excommunication
13 *becks* beckons   17 *Coz* kinsman   21 *creditor* debtor   22 *advantage* interest; *pay* repay   23 *voluntary* freely offered

Give me thy hand. I had a thing to say,
But I will fit it with some better tune.
By heaven, Hubert, I am almost ashamed
28   To say what good respect I have of thee.

HUBERT

29   I am much bounden to your majesty.

KING JOHN

30   Good friend, thou hast no cause to say so yet,
But thou shalt have; and creep time ne'er so slow,
Yet it shall come for me to do thee good.
I had a thing to say, but let it go.
The sun is in the heaven, and the proud day,
35   Attended with the pleasures of the world,
36   Is all too wanton and too full of gawds
37   To give me audience. If the midnight bell
38   Did with his iron tongue and brazen mouth
Sound on into the drowsy ear of night;
40   If this same were a churchyard where we stand,
41   And thou possessèd with a thousand wrongs;
Or if that surly spirit, melancholy,
Had baked thy blood and made it heavy, thick,
44   Which else runs tickling up and down the veins,
Making that idiot, laughter, keep men's eyes
And strain their cheeks to idle merriment,
A passion hateful to my purposes;
Or if that thou couldst see me without eyes,
Hear me without thine ears, and make reply
50   Without a tongue, using conceit alone,
Without eyes, ears, and harmful sound of words;
52   Then, in despite of broad-eyed watchful day,

---

28 *respect* opinion   29 *bounden* obliged   35 *Attended with* accompanied by
36 *gawds* showy ornaments, such as the flowers in springtime   37 *To . . . au-*
dience to listen to me   38 *brazen* brass   41 *possessèd with* bearer of, owner of
44 *tickling* tingling   50 *conceit* imagination   52 *broad-eyed* with eyes wide
open

I would into thy bosom pour my thoughts.
But ah, I will not. Yet I love thee well,
And, by my troth, I think thou lov'st me well.   55

HUBERT
So well, that what you bid me undertake,
Though that my death were adjunct to my act,   57
By heaven, I would do it.

KING JOHN   Do not I know thou wouldst?
Good Hubert! Hubert, Hubert, throw thine eye   59
On yon young boy. I'll tell thee what, my friend,   60
He is a very serpent in my way,
And wheresoe'er this foot of mine doth tread
He lies before me. Dost thou understand me?
Thou art his keeper.

HUBERT   And I'll keep him so
That he shall not offend your majesty.

KING JOHN
Death.

HUBERT   My lord?

KING JOHN   A grave.

HUBERT   He shall not live.

KING JOHN   Enough.
I could be merry now. Hubert, I love thee.
Well, I'll not say what I intend for thee.
Remember. Madam, fare you well.
I'll send those powers o'er to your majesty.   70

ELEANOR
My blessing go with thee!

KING JOHN   For England, cousin, go.
Hubert shall be your man, attend on you   72
With all true duty. On toward Calais, ho!   *Exeunt.*

*

---

55 *by my troth* (1) by my truth, (2) I would swear   57 *adjunct to* the result of
59 *throw* cast   70 *powers* troops   72 *man* servant; *attend* wait

∾ **III.4** *Enter [King Philip of] France, [Lewis the] Dauphin, Pandulph, Attendants.*

KING PHILIP

1 So by a roaring tempest on the flood,
2 A whole armado of convicted sail
    Is scattered and disjoined from fellowship.

PANDULPH

    Courage and comfort! All shall yet go well.

KING PHILIP

5 What can go well when we have run so ill?
    Are we not beaten? Is not Angiers lost?
7 Arthur ta'en prisoner? Divers dear friends slain?
8 And bloody England into England gone,
9 O'erbearing interruption, spite of France?

LEWIS

10 What he hath won, that hath he fortified.
11 So hot a speed with such advice disposed,
12 Such temperate order in so fierce a cause,
13 Doth want example. Who hath read or heard
14 Of any kindred action like to this?

KING PHILIP

    Well could I bear that England had this praise,
16 So we could find some pattern of our shame.
    Enter Constance.
    Look, who comes here! A grave unto a soul,
    Holding th' eternal spirit, against her will,
19 In the vile prison of afflicted breath.
20 I prithee, lady, go away with me.

III.4 The French camp   **1** *flood* ocean   **2** *armado* fleet of warships; *convicted sail* doomed ships   **5** *run so ill* fared so badly   **7** *Divers* several   **8** *England . . . gone* i.e., King John gone into England   **9** *O'erbearing* despite; *interruption* resistance; *spite of* despite   **10** *fortified* reinforced, secured   **11** *with such advice disposed* controlled with such good judgment   **12** *temperate* calm   **13** *Doth want example* is without precedent   **14** *kindred* similar   **16** *So* if; *pattern* example in the past   **19** *breath* life

CONSTANCE
    Lo, now! Now see the issue of your peace!
KING PHILIP
    Patience, good lady! Comfort, gentle Constance!
CONSTANCE
    No, I defy all counsel, all redress,   23
    But that which ends all counsel, true redress,
    Death, death. O, amiable, lovely death!
    Thou odoriferous stench! Sound rottenness!   26
    Arise forth from the couch of lasting night,   27
    Thou hate and terror to prosperity,
    And I will kiss thy detestable bones,
    And put my eyeballs in thy vaulty brows,   30
    And ring these fingers with thy household worms,
    And stop this gap of breath with fulsome dust,   32
    And be a carrion monster like thyself.
    Come, grin on me, and I will think thou smil'st
    And buss thee as thy wife! Misery's love,   35
    O, come to me!
KING PHILIP   O fair affliction, peace!
CONSTANCE
    No, no, I will not, having breath to cry.   37
    O that my tongue were in the thunder's mouth!
    Then with a passion would I shake the world,
    And rouse from sleep that fell anatomy   40
    Which cannot hear a lady's feeble voice,
    Which scorns a modern invocation.   42
PANDULPH
    Lady, you utter madness and not sorrow.
CONSTANCE
    Thou art not holy to belie me so.   44
    I am not mad; this hair I tear is mine.

_____

23 *defy* reject 26 *odoriferous* fragrant 27 *lasting* everlasting 30 *vaulty*
arched 32 *stop . . . breath* stop up his mouth; *fulsome* physically disgusting
35 *buss* kiss 37 *cry* (1) weep, (2) cry out, complain 40 *fell anatomy* cruel
skeleton (as death traditionally was personified) 42 *modern invocation* ordinary supplication 44 *belie* slander

My name is Constance; I was Geoffrey's wife.
Young Arthur is my son, and he is lost!
I am not mad. I would to God I were,
49 For then 'tis like I should forget myself.
50 O, if I could, what grief should I forget!
Preach some philosophy to make me mad,
And thou shalt be canonized, cardinal.
53 For, being not mad but sensible of grief,
My reasonable part produces reason
55 How I may be delivered of these woes,
And teaches me to kill or hang myself.
If I were mad, I should forget my son,
58 Or madly think a babe of clouts were he.
I am not mad. Too well, too well I feel
60 The different plague of each calamity.

KING PHILIP
Bind up those tresses. O, what love I note
In the fair multitude of those her hairs!
63 Where but by chance a silver drop hath fallen,
64 Even to that drop ten thousand wiry friends
65 Do glue themselves in sociable grief,
Like true, inseparable, faithful loves,
Sticking together in calamity.

CONSTANCE
68 To England, if you will.

KING PHILIP   Bind up your hairs.

CONSTANCE
69 Yes, that I will; and wherefore will I do it?
70 I tore them from their bonds and cried aloud:

---

49 *like* probable 53 *sensible* capable 55 *be delivered of* give birth to, separate myself from (Constance sees death as her lover, grief as her child) 58
babe of clouts rag doll 63 *silver drop* tear 64 *wiry friends* hairs (wire was a
common metaphor for hair) 65 *sociable* sympathetic 68 *To England . . .
will* (a line that is usually taken as evidence of some revision in this scene,
since it bears no relation to its immediate context, but may be an answer to
King Philip's invitation at line 20) 69 *wherefore* why

"O that these hands could so redeem my son,   71
As they have given these hairs their liberty!"
But now I envy at their liberty,   73
And will again commit them to their bonds,
Because my poor child is a prisoner.
    [She binds her hair.]
And, Father Cardinal, I have heard you say
That we shall see and know our friends in heaven.
If that be true, I shall see my boy again,
For since the birth of Cain, the first male child,   79
To him that did but yesterday suspire,   80
There was not such a gracious creature born.   81
But now will canker sorrow eat my bud   82
And chase the native beauty from his cheek,   83
And he will look as hollow as a ghost,
As dim and meager as an ague's fit,   85
And so he'll die; and rising so again,   86
When I shall meet him in the court of heaven
I shall not know him. Therefore never, never
Must I behold my pretty Arthur more.

PANDULPH
You hold too heinous a respect of grief.   90
CONSTANCE
He talks to me that never had a son.
KING PHILIP
You are as fond of grief as of your child.   92
CONSTANCE
Grief fills the room up of my absent child,   93

---

71 *redeem* (1) ransom, (2) rescue   73 *envy at* begrudge   79 *Cain* eldest son
of Adam and Eve, and – strangely, in this context – murderer of his brother
Abel (the sense of 79–81 is that Arthur is unparalleled in the world's history
of sons)   80 *suspire* breathe   81 *gracious* meriting divine grace, destined for
heaven   82 *canker* like a canker worm (which destroys plants); *my bud* i.e.,
Arthur   83 *native* natural, innate   85 *dim* pale; *ague's fit* tremors caused by
fever   86 *rising so* i.e., rising from the dead into heaven   90 *heinous a respect*
terrible an opinion   92 *fond of* foolishly infatuated with   93 *fills . . . up*
takes the place of

Lies in his bed, walks up and down with me,
Puts on his pretty looks, repeats his words,
96 Remembers me of all his gracious parts,
97 Stuffs out his vacant garments with his form.
Then have I reason to be fond of grief.
Fare you well. Had you such a loss as I,
100 I could give better comfort than you do.
     [She unbinds her hair.]
101 I will not keep this form upon my head,
102 When there is such disorder in my wit.
O Lord! My boy, my Arthur, my fair son!
My life, my joy, my food, my all the world!
My widow-comfort, and my sorrows' cure!   *Exit.*

KING PHILIP
106 I fear some outrage, and I'll follow her.   *Exit.*

LEWIS
107 There's nothing in this world can make me joy.
Life is as tedious as a twice-told tale,
Vexing the dull ear of a drowsy man,
110 And bitter shame hath spoiled the sweet word's taste,
111 That it yields nought but shame and bitterness.

PANDULPH
Before the curing of a strong disease,
113 Even in the instant of repair and health,
The fit is strongest. Evils that take leave,
115 On their departure most of all show evil.
116 What have you lost by losing of this day?

LEWIS
All days of glory, joy, and happiness.

PANDULPH
If you had won it, certainly you had.

---

96 *Remembers* reminds   **97** *his form* i.e., grief's   **101** *form* orderly arrangement of hair   **102** *wit* mind   **106** *outrage* injury (to herself)   **107** *joy* rejoice   **111** *nought* nothing   **113** *Even ... instant* at the very moment; *repair* recovery   **115** *On* upon   **116** *day* day of battle

No, no; when Fortune means to men most good,
She looks upon them with a threat'ning eye.   120
'Tis strange to think how much King John hath lost
In this which he accounts so clearly won.   122
Are not you grieved that Arthur is his prisoner?

LEWIS
As heartily as he is glad he hath him.

PANDULPH
Your mind is all as youthful as your blood.   125
Now hear me speak with a prophetic spirit,
For even the breath of what I mean to speak
Shall blow each dust, each straw, each little rub,   128
Out of the path which shall directly lead
Thy foot to England's throne. And therefore mark: 130
John hath seized Arthur, and it cannot be
That, whiles warm life plays in that infant's veins,
The misplaced John should entertain an hour,   133
One minute, nay, one quiet breath of rest.
A scepter snatched with an unruly hand
Must be as boisterously maintained as gained,   136
And he that stands upon a slippery place
Makes nice of no vile hold to stay him up.   138
That John may stand, then Arthur needs must fall;
So be it, for it cannot be but so.   140

LEWIS
But what shall I gain by young Arthur's fall?

PANDULPH
You, in the right of Lady Blanche your wife,   142
May then make all the claim that Arthur did.

LEWIS
And lose it, life and all, as Arthur did.

---

122 *accounts* esteems, judges; *clearly* obviously, easily   125 *youthful . . .
blood* immature as your actual age (?)   128 *dust* grain of dust; *rub* obstacle
(in the game of bowls)   130 *mark* remark, note   133 *misplaced* usurping
136 *boisterously* violently   138 *Makes . . . up* is not scrupulous about what
evil means he uses to support himself   142 *in the right* through the claim

PANDULPH

145 How green you are and fresh in this old world!
146 John lays you plots; the times conspire with you,
147 For he that steeps his safety in true blood
Shall find but bloody safety and untrue.
149 This act so evilly borne shall cool the hearts
150 Of all his people and freeze up their zeal,
151 That none so small advantage shall step forth
152 To check his reign, but they will cherish it;
153 No natural exhalation in the sky,
154 No scope of nature, no distempered day,
155 No common wind, no customèd event,
156 But they will pluck away his natural cause
157 And call them meteors, prodigies, and signs,
158 Abortives, presages, and tongues of heaven,
Plainly denouncing vengeance upon John.

LEWIS

160 May be he will not touch young Arthur's life,
161 But hold himself safe in his prisonment.

PANDULPH

O, sir, when he shall hear of your approach,
If that young Arthur be not gone already,
164 Even at that news he dies; and then the hearts
165 Of all his people shall revolt from him
166 And kiss the lips of unacquainted change,
167 And pick strong matter of revolt and wrath

---

145 *green* inexperienced   146 *lays you plots* makes plans for your advantage   147–48 *he . . . untrue* he who bases his safety on his killing of the true king (Arthur) will find his safety bloody and false   149 *so evilly borne* carried out so wickedly   150 *zeal* enthusiasm   151 *advantage* opportunity   152 *check* obstruct   153 *exhalation* meteor   154 *scope of nature* a seemingly impossible event, which is nevertheless within the possibility of nature; *distempered* full of bad weather   155 *customèd* ordinary   156 *his* its   157 *prodigies* portents   158 *Abortives* (1) miscarriages, (2) monstrous and untimely progeny; *presages* predictions; *tongues of heaven* divine judgments   161 *himself* i.e., John; *safe* secure upon the throne   164 *he* i.e., Arthur   165 *his* i.e., John's   166 *kiss . . . change* be enamored of any new change   167–68 *pick . . . John* find cause for revolt and anger in John's bloody deeds

Out of the bloody fingers' ends of John.
Methinks I see this hurly all on foot;   169
And, O, what better matter breeds for you   170
Than I have named! The bastard Faulconbridge
Is now in England ransacking the church,
Offending charity. If but a dozen French   173
Were there in arms, they would be as a call   174
To train ten thousand English to their side,   175
Or as a little snow, tumbled about,
Anon becomes a mountain. O noble dauphin,   177
Go with me to the king. 'Tis wonderful
What may be wrought out of their discontent,
Now that their souls are topful of offense.   180
For England go; I will whet on the king.   181

LEWIS
Strong reasons make strange actions. Let us go.
If you say ay, the king will not say no.   *Exeunt.*   183

*

∾ **IV.1** *Enter Hubert and Executioners.*

HUBERT
Heat me these irons hot, and look thou stand
Within the arras. When I strike my foot   2
Upon the bosom of the ground, rush forth   3
And bind the boy which you shall find with me
Fast to the chair. Be heedful. Hence, and watch.

[FIRST] EXECUTIONER
I hope your warrant will bear out the deed.   6

---

169 *hurly* commotion; *on foot* started   170 *breeds* is ripening   173 *charity* good will   174 *call* decoy (as a birdcall)   175 *train* attract   177 *Anon* soon 180 *topful of offense* filled to the brim with grievances   181 *whet on* incite 183 *ay* yes

IV.1 Arthur's prison   2 *Within the arras* behind the wall hanging   3 *bosom* surface   6 *warrant* order (to execute Arthur); *bear out* be sufficient to justify

HUBERT

7   Uncleanly scruples! Fear not you. Look to 't.

>   [Exeunt Executioners.]

8   Young lad, come forth; I have to say with you.

Enter Arthur.

ARTHUR

Good morrow, Hubert.

HUBERT   Good morrow, little prince.

ARTHUR

10   As little prince, having so great a title

To be more prince, as may be. You are sad.

HUBERT

Indeed, I have been merrier.

ARTHUR   Mercy on me!

Methinks nobody should be sad but I.

Yet I remember, when I was in France

15   Young gentlemen would be as sad as night,

16   Only for wantonness. By my Christendom,

17   So I were out of prison and kept sheep,

I should be as merry as the day is long;

19   And so I would be here, but that I doubt

20   My uncle practices more harm to me.

He is afraid of me and I of him.

Is it my fault that I was Geoffrey's son?

No, indeed, is 't not, and I would to God

I were your son, so you would love me, Hubert.

HUBERT   *[Aside]*

25   If I talk to him, with his innocent prate

He will awake my mercy which lies dead;

---

7 *Uncleanly* improper, unbecoming; *Fear not you* don't you worry   **8** *to say with* something to say to   **10–11** *As . . . may be* as little of a prince (since I am in captivity) as one with my great title possibly could be   **15–16** *as sad . . . wantonness* melancholy merely as a whimsical affectation (a common pose among gentlemen of Shakespeare's day)   **16** *Christendom* baptism, hence faith as a Christian   **17** *So* if; *kept sheep* i.e., as a shepherd (conventionally imagined to be free from all worldly cares)   **19** *doubt* fear   **20** *practices* plots   **25** *prate* prattle

Therefore I will be sudden and dispatch.   27

ARTHUR
Are you sick, Hubert? You look pale today.
In sooth, I would you were a little sick,   29
That I might sit all night and watch with you.   30
I warrant I love you more than you do me.   31

HUBERT   *[Aside]*
His words do take possession of my bosom.
Read here, young Arthur. *[Shows a paper.]*   33
     [Aside]   How now, foolish rheum,
Turning dispiteous torture out of door!   34
I must be brief, lest resolution drop
Out at mine eyes in tender womanish tears.
Can you not read it? Is it not fair writ?   37

ARTHUR
Too fairly, Hubert, for so foul effect.   38
Must you with hot irons burn out both mine eyes?

HUBERT
Young boy, I must.   40

ARTHUR   And will you?

HUBERT   And I will.

ARTHUR
Have you the heart? When your head did but ache,
I knit my handkerchief about your brows –
The best I had, a princess wrought it me –   43
And I did never ask it you again;   44
And with my hand at midnight held your head,
And like the watchful minutes to the hour,   46
Still and anon cheered up the heavy time,   47

---

27 *dispatch* do the job quickly   29 *sooth* truth   30 *with* over   31 *warrant*
declare   33 *rheum* tears   34 *dispiteous* merciless   37 *fair writ* clearly written
38 *effect* purpose   40 *And I will* if I will   43 *wrought it me* embroidered it
for me   44 *ask it you* ask you to return it   46 *watchful . . . hour* minutes that
mark the progress of the hour   47 *Still and anon* continually from time to
time (Arthur compares his questions to the ticking of the minutes, which
makes the hour go by more quickly); *heavy* dreary

48   Saying, "What lack you?" and "Where lies your grief?"
49   Or "What good love may I perform for you?"
50   Many a poor man's son would have lain still,
      And ne'er have spoke a loving word to you,
52   But you at your sick service had a prince.
53   Nay, you may think my love was crafty love,
      And call it cunning; do and if you will.
55   If heaven be pleased that you must use me ill,
      Why then you must. Will you put out mine eyes?
      These eyes that never did nor never shall
      So much as frown on you?

HUBERT   I have sworn to do it,
      And with hot irons must I burn them out.

ARTHUR
60   Ah, none but in this iron age would do it!
61   The iron of itself, though heat red-hot,
      Approaching near these eyes, would drink my tears
      And quench this fiery indignation
64   Even in the matter of mine innocence,
      Nay, after that, consume away in rust,
66   But for containing fire to harm mine eye.
      Are you more stubborn-hard than hammered iron?
      And if an angel should have come to me
      And told me Hubert should put out mine eyes,
70   I would not have believed him – no tongue but Hubert's.

HUBERT   *[Stamps.]*
      Come forth.
        [Enter Executioners, with a cord, irons, etc.]
      Do as I bid you do.

---

48 *Where lies your grief* (1) where does it hurt, (2) what troubles you   49 *love* service, comfort   52 *at your sick service* at your service (as a nurse) when you were sick   53 *crafty* pretended   55 *use me ill* treat me badly   60 *iron age* cruel, degenerate present (as opposed to the heroic golden age of antiquity)   61 *heat* heated   64 *matter of mine innocence* tears, the signs of innocence   66 *But* merely

ARTHUR

   O! save me, Hubert, save me! My eyes are out
   Even with the fierce looks of these bloody men.

HUBERT

   Give me the iron, I say, and bind him here.

ARTHUR

   Alas, what need you be so boist'rous rough?   76
   I will not struggle, I will stand stone still.
   For heaven sake, Hubert, let me not be bound!
   Nay, hear me, Hubert! Drive these men away,
   And I will sit as quiet as a lamb.   80
   I will not stir, nor wince, nor speak a word,
   Nor look upon the iron angrily.
   Thrust but these men away, and I'll forgive you,
   Whatever torment you do put me to.

HUBERT

   Go, stand within. Let me alone with him.   85

[FIRST] EXECUTIONER

   I am best pleased to be from such a deed.   86

                        [Exeunt Executioners.]

ARTHUR

   Alas! I then have chid away my friend!   87
   He hath a stern look but a gentle heart.
   Let him come back, that his compassion may
   Give life to yours.   90

HUBERT   Come, boy, prepare yourself.

ARTHUR

   Is there no remedy?

HUBERT   None, but to lose your eyes.

ARTHUR

   O heaven, that there were but a mote in yours,   92
   A grain, a dust, a gnat, a wandering hair,
   Any annoyance in that precious sense.

---

76 *what* why   85 *Let . . . him* leave me to deal with him alone   86 *from*
away from   87 *chid* driven off, scolded away; *my friend* i.e., the executioner
92 *mote* speck of dust

95   Then feeling what small things are boisterous there,
       Your vile intent must needs seem horrible.

HUBERT
97   Is this your promise? Go to, hold your tongue.

ARTHUR
98   Hubert, the utterance of a brace of tongues
99   Must needs want pleading for a pair of eyes.
100   Let me not hold my tongue, let me not, Hubert;
       Or, Hubert, if you will, cut out my tongue,
       So I may keep mine eyes. O, spare mine eyes,
103   Though to no use but still to look on you!
104   Lo, by my troth, the instrument is cold
       And would not harm me.

HUBERT   I can heat it, boy.

ARTHUR
       No, in good sooth. The fire is dead with grief,
107   Being create for comfort, to be used
108   In undeserved extremes. See else yourself.
       There is no malice in this burning coal.
110   The breath of heaven hath blown his spirit out
       And strewed repentant ashes on his head.

HUBERT
       But with my breath I can revive it, boy.

ARTHUR
       And if you do, you will but make it blush
114   And glow with shame of your proceedings, Hubert.
115   Nay, it perchance will sparkle in your eyes,
       And like a dog that is compelled to fight,
117   Snatch at his master that doth tarre him on.
       All things that you should use to do me wrong
119   Deny their office. Only you do lack

---

95 *boisterous* irritating; *there* in one's eyes   97 *Go to* (a protestation)   **98–99**
the utterance . . . pleading even two tongues (*brace:* a pair) could not plead
adequately   99 *want* lack   103 *still* always   104 *troth* faith   107 *create* created   108 *In undeserved extremes* to inflict undeserved acts of cruelty   114
of at   115 *sparkle* throw out sparks   117 *tarre* provoke to fight   119 *Deny
their office* refuse to perform their proper function

That mercy which fierce fire and iron extends,   120
Creatures of note for mercy-lacking uses.   121

HUBERT
Well, see to live; I will not touch thine eye
For all the treasure that thine uncle owns.
Yet am I sworn and I did purpose, boy,   124
With this same very iron to burn them out.

ARTHUR
O, now you look like Hubert! All this while
You were disguisèd.

HUBERT   Peace! No more. Adieu.
Your uncle must not know but you are dead.   128
I'll fill these doggèd spies with false reports.   129
And, pretty child, sleep doubtless and secure   130
That Hubert for the wealth of all the world
Will not offend thee.

ARTHUR   O heaven! I thank you, Hubert.

HUBERT
Silence! No more! Go closely in with me.   133
Much danger do I undergo for thee.   *Exeunt.*

*

∾ **IV.2** *Enter [King] John, Pembroke, Salisbury, and
other Lords.*

KING JOHN
Here once again we sit, once again crowned,   1
And looked upon, I hope, with cheerful eyes.

PEMBROKE
This "once again," but that your highness pleased,   3

---

120 *extends* exhibit   **121** *Creatures* i.e., fire and iron; *of note . . . uses* noted
for their customary use in cruel affairs   **124** *purpose* intend   **128** *but* other
than that   **129** *doggèd* malicious   **130** *doubtless* without fear; *secure* assured
133 *closely* secretly

IV.2 The English court   **1** *once again* (John has just had himself re-
crowned to mark the end of his domination by the church of Rome)   **3**
pleased wished it

4   Was once superfluous. You were crowned before,
    And that high royalty was ne'er plucked off,
6   The faiths of men ne'er stainèd with revolt.
7   Fresh expectation troubled not the land
8   With any longed-for change or better state.
SALISBURY
9   Therefore, to be possessed with double pomp,
10 To guard a title that was rich before,
    To gild refinèd gold, to paint the lily,
    To throw a perfume on the violet,
    To smooth the ice, or add another hue
14 Unto the rainbow, or with taper light
    To seek the beauteous eye of heaven to garnish,
    Is wasteful and ridiculous excess.
PEMBROKE
17 But that your royal pleasure must be done,
    This act is as an ancient tale new told,
19 And in the last repeating troublesome,
20 Being urgèd at a time unseasonable.
SALISBURY
21 In this the antique and well-noted face
22 Of plain old form is much disfigured,
23 And like a shifted wind unto a sail,
24 It makes the course of thoughts to fetch about,
25 Startles and frights consideration,
    Makes sound opinion sick and truth suspected,
    For putting on so new a fashioned robe.

---

4 *once superfluous* one time too many (unnecessary) 6 *stainèd* corrupted
7 *expectation* excited anticipation of change 8 *state* government 9 *with* of;
pomp solemn ceremony (coronation) 10 *guard* ornament a garment with
trimmings 14–15 *with taper light . . . garnish* to try to add to the sun's
beauty by means of candlelight 17 *But that* except for that 19 *repeating*
repetition 20 *unseasonable* inconvenient 21 *antique* ancient; *well-noted*
well-known 22 *plain old form* simple customary behavior 23 *shifted wind*
change of wind 24 *It* i.e., the second coronation; *fetch about* change their
direction 25 *consideration* thought (about the succession; by a second coronation John is causing others to question the validity of his title)

PEMBROKE

When workmen strive to do better than well,
They do confound their skill in covetousness,   29
And oftentimes excusing of a fault   30
Doth make the fault the worse by the excuse,
As patches set upon a little breach   32
Discredit more in hiding of the fault   33
Than did the fault before it was so patched.

SALISBURY

To this effect, before you were new crowned,
We breathed our counsel, but it pleased your highness   36
To overbear it, and we are all well pleased,   37
Since all and every part of what we would   38
Doth make a stand at what your highness will.

KING JOHN

Some reasons of this double coronation   40
I have possessed you with and think them strong;   41
And more, more strong, when lesser is my fear,   42
I shall indue you with. Meantime but ask   43
What you would have reformed that is not well,
And well shall you perceive how willingly
I will both hear and grant you your requests.

PEMBROKE

Then I, as one that am the tongue of these   47
To sound the purposes of all their hearts,   48
Both for myself and them – but, chief of all,
Your safety, for the which myself and them   50
Bend their best studies – heartily request   51

---

29 *confound . . . covetousness* destroy what they have done well by their desire
to do even better **32** *breach* hole in a garment **33** *fault* defect **36**
breathed spoke **37** *overbear* veto by superior power **38–39** *Since . . . will*
since our wishes can never run counter to your desires **40** *of* for **41** *possessed you with* informed you of **42** *more* i.e., more such reasons **43** *indue*
furnish **47** *these* i.e., these others **48** *sound the purposes* express the propos-
als **50** *them* they **51** *Bend their best studies* direct their most diligent efforts

52   Th' enfranchisement of Arthur, whose restraint
      Doth move the murmuring lips of discontent
      To break into this dangerous argument:
55   If what in rest you have in right you hold,
56   Why then your fears, which, as they say, attend
57   The steps of wrong, should move you to mew up
58   Your tender kinsman, and to choke his days
      With barbarous ignorance and deny his youth
60   The rich advantage of good exercise.
61   That the time's enemies may not have this
62   To grace occasions, let it be our suit
      That you have bid us ask, his liberty,
64   Which for our goods we do no further ask
65   Than whereupon our weal, on you depending,
      Counts it your weal he have his liberty.
        Enter Hubert.

KING JOHN
67   Let it be so. I do commit his youth
      To your direction. Hubert, what news with you?
        [Takes him apart.]

PEMBROKE
69   This is the man should do the bloody deed;
70   He showed his warrant to a friend of mine.
71   The image of a wicked heinous fault
72   Lives in his eye. That close aspect of his
      Does show the mood of a much troubled breast,
      And I do fearfully believe 'tis done,
75   What we so feared he had a charge to do.

---

52 *enfranchisement* release from prison; *restraint* imprisonment **55** *If . . . hold* if you hold rightfully what you possess peaceably **56–57** *attend . . . wrong* accompany wrongdoing **57** *mew up* shut up **58** *tender* youthful **58–59** *choke . . . ignorance* keep him from useful study **60** *exercise* education of a gentleman **61** *time's enemies* those opposed to the present state of affairs **62** *grace occasions* make proper and acceptable their opportunities to attack **64** *our goods* our own good **65** *whereupon* to the extent that; *weal* welfare **67–68** *commit . . . direction* put him and his education under your supervision **69** *should* who should **71** *image* reflection **72** *close aspect* secret expression **75** *charge* order

SALISBURY

   The color of the king doth come and go   76
   Between his purpose and his conscience,
   Like heralds 'twixt two dreadful battles set.   78
   His passion is so ripe it needs must break.   79

PEMBROKE

   And when it breaks, I fear will issue thence   80
   The foul corruption of a sweet child's death.   81

KING JOHN

   We cannot hold mortality's strong hand.   82
   Good lords, although my will to give is living,   83
   The suit which you demand is gone and dead.   84
   He tells us Arthur is deceased tonight.

SALISBURY

   Indeed we feared his sickness was past cure.

PEMBROKE

   Indeed we heard how near his death he was,
   Before the child himself felt he was sick.
   This must be answered either here or hence.   89

KING JOHN

   Why do you bend such solemn brows on me?   90
   Think you I bear the shears of destiny?   91
   Have I commandment on the pulse of life?

SALISBURY

   It is apparent foul play, and 'tis shame
   That greatness should so grossly offer it.   94
   So thrive it in your game! And so, farewell.   95

PEMBROKE

   Stay yet, Lord Salisbury. I'll go with thee

---

76 *color* i.e., of his complexion (with a pun on "battle flag")   78 *battles* armies arranged for battle; *set* assigned to perform duties   79 *break* burst open (like a boil)   81 *corruption* pus   82 *hold* stay, prevent   83 *my . . . living* my desire to agree to your request remains   84 *suit* request   89 *answered* accounted or atoned for; *here or hence* in this world or the next   90 *bend . . . brows* frown   91 *shears of destiny* instrument with which Atropos, one of the three Fates, cuts the thread of life   94 *That . . . offer it* that a king should act so outrageously   95 *So . . . game* may you suffer accordingly

97   And find th' inheritance of this poor child,
98   His little kingdom of a forcèd grave.
99   That blood which owned the breadth of all this isle,
100   Three foot of it doth hold – bad world the while!
101   This must not be thus borne. This will break out
102   To all our sorrows, and ere long, I doubt.

Exeunt [Lords].

KING JOHN
      They burn in indignation. I repent.
          Enter Messenger.
104   There is no sure foundation set on blood,
      No certain life achieved by others' death.
106   A fearful eye thou hast. Where is that blood
      That I have seen inhabit in those cheeks?
      So foul a sky clears not without a storm.
109   Pour down thy weather. How goes all in France?

MESSENGER
110 From France to England. Never such a power
111   For any foreign preparation
112   Was levied in the body of a land.
113   The copy of your speed is learned by them,
      For when you should be told they do prepare,
115   The tidings comes that they are all arrived.

KING JOHN
116   O, where hath our intelligence been drunk?
      Where hath it slept? Where is my mother's care,
118   That such an army could be drawn in France,
119   And she not hear of it?

---

97 *th' inheritance* (1) the remains, (2) the resting place   98 *forcèd* imposed by violence   99 *blood* life   100 *the while* when such things happen   101 *borne* tolerated; *break out* have consequences   102 *ere* before; *doubt* fear   104 *set on blood* built on violence   106 *fearful* full of fear   109 *weather* (1) tempest, (2) bad news   111 *preparation* expedition (pronounced as five syllables) 112 *levied in* raised from   113 *copy* example; *learned* imitated   115 *arrived* landed   116 *intelligence* spy system   118 *drawn* mustered   119–23 *her ear . . . before* (Queen Eleanor actually died on April 1, 1204; Constance died in 1201)

MESSENGER   My liege, her ear
  Is stopped with dust. The first of April died   *120*
  Your noble mother; and, as I hear, my lord,
  The Lady Constance in a frenzy died
  Three days before. But this from rumor's tongue
  I idly heard; if true or false I know not.   *124*

KING JOHN
  Withhold thy speed, dreadful occasion!   *125*
  O, make a league with me, till I have pleased   *126*
  My discontented peers. What! Mother dead!
  How wildly then walks my estate in France!   *128*
  Under whose conduct came those powers of France   *129*
  That thou for truth giv'st out are landed here?   *130*

MESSENGER
  Under the dauphin.

KING JOHN   Thou hast made me giddy
  With these ill tidings.
      Enter Bastard and Peter of Pomfret.
                            Now, what says the world
  To your proceedings? Do not seek to stuff
  My head with more ill news, for it is full.

BASTARD
  But if you be afeard to hear the worst,
  Then let the worst unheard fall on your head.

KING JOHN
  Bear with me, cousin, for I was amazed   *137*
  Under the tide; but now I breathe again   *138*
  Aloft the flood and can give audience   *139*
  To any tongue, speak it of what it will.   *140*

BASTARD
  How I have sped among the clergymen   *141*
  The sums I have collected shall express.

---

124 *idly* without paying full attention   125 *occasion* course of events   126
league alliance   128 *wildly* randomly; *walks* proceeds; *estate* concerns, affairs
129 *conduct* leadership   130 *for . . . out* as the true report   137 *amazed* bewildered   138 *tide* i.e., of bad news   139 *Aloft* above; *give audience* listen
141 *sped* fared

But as I traveled hither through the land,
144   I find the people strangely fantasied,
145   Possessed with rumors, full of idle dreams,
Not knowing what they fear, but full of fear.
And here's a prophet that I brought with me
148   From forth the streets of Pomfret, whom I found
149   With many hundreds treading on his heels,
150   To whom he sung, in rude harsh-sounding rhymes,
151   That ere the next Ascension Day at noon,
Your highness should deliver up your crown.

KING JOHN
153   Thou idle dreamer, wherefore didst thou so?

PETER
154   Foreknowing that the truth will fall out so.

KING JOHN
Hubert, away with him; imprison him,
And on that day at noon, whereon he says
I shall yield up my crown, let him be hanged.
158   Deliver him to safety and return,
159   For I must use thee.   *[Exit Hubert, with Peter.]*
                              O my gentle cousin,
160   Hear'st thou the news abroad, who are arrived?

BASTARD
The French, my lord. Men's mouths are full of it.
Besides, I met Lord Bigot and Lord Salisbury,
With eyes as red as new-enkindled fire,
And others more, going to seek the grave
Of Arthur, whom they say is killed tonight
On your suggestion.

KING JOHN   Gentle kinsman, go,
167   And thrust thyself into their companies.

---

144 *strangely fantasied* full of strange notions   145 *Possessed with* controlled by   148 *Pomfret* Pontefract in Yorkshire   149 *on* at   151 *Ascension Day* the day forty days after Easter when Christ ascended to heaven (and the day of the year from which King John's reign was reckoned)   153 *idle* foolish   154 *fall out* occur   158 *safety* safekeeping   159 *gentle* courteous, kind   167 *thrust . . . companies* associate with them

I have a way to win their loves again.
Bring them before me.
BASTARD   I will seek them out.
KING JOHN
Nay, but make haste, the better foot before.   170
O, let me have no subject enemies,   171
When adverse foreigners affright my towns   172
With dreadful pomp of stout invasion.   173
Be Mercury, set feathers to thy heels,   174
And fly like thought from them to me again.
BASTARD
The spirit of the time shall teach me speed.   *Exit.*
KING JOHN
Spoke like a sprightful noble gentleman.   177
Go after him, for he perhaps shall need
Some messenger betwixt me and the peers;
And be thou he.   180
MESSENGER   With all my heart, my liege.   *[Exit.]*
KING JOHN
My mother dead!
    Enter Hubert.
HUBERT
My lord, they say five moons were seen tonight –   182
Four fixèd, and the fifth did whirl about
The other four in wondrous motion.   184
KING JOHN
Five moons!   185
HUBERT   Old men and beldams in the streets
Do prophesy upon it dangerously.   186

---

170 *better foot* i.e., quickly   171 *subject enemies* i.e., rebel subjects or citizens
172 *adverse* hostile   173 *dreadful* causing dread; *pomp* ceremony, show; *stout*
bold   174 *Mercury* the messenger of the gods, who wore winged sandals
177 *sprightful* full of spirit   182 *five moons* (a type of unnatural phenomenon believed to herald disaster to a kingdom); *tonight* i.e., last night   184
wondrous i.e., causing wonder   185 *beldams* hags   186 *prophesy upon it* attempt to explain the unnatural phenomenon; *dangerously* (1) ominously, (2)
daringly

187 Young Arthur's death is common in their mouths,
     And when they talk of him, they shake their heads
189 And whisper one another in the ear;
190 And he that speaks doth gripe the hearer's wrist,
191 Whilst he that hears makes fearful action,
     With wrinkled brows, with nods, with rolling eyes.
193 I saw a smith stand with his hammer, thus,
     The whilst his iron did on the anvil cool,
195 With open mouth swallowing a tailor's news;
196 Who, with his shears and measure in his hand,
197 Standing on slippers, which his nimble haste
198 Had falsely thrust upon contrary feet,
     Told of a many thousand warlike French,
200 That were embattailèd and ranked in Kent.
201 Another lean unwashed artificer
202 Cuts off his tale and talks of Arthur's death.

KING JOHN
     Why seek'st thou to possess me with these fears?
     Why urgest thou so oft young Arthur's death?
205 Thy hand hath murdered him. I had a mighty cause
     To wish him dead, but thou hadst none to kill him.

HUBERT
207 No had, my lord? Why, did you not provoke me?

KING JOHN
208 It is the curse of kings to be attended
209 By slaves that take their humors for a warrant
210 To break within the bloody house of life,
211 And on the winking of authority

---

187 *common . . . mouths* i.e., everyone speaks of it   189 *whisper one* whisper to one   191 *action* gestures   193 *smith* blacksmith   195 *open* i.e., gaping; *swallowing* devouring   196 *measure* measuring stick   197 *on* in   198 *contrary* wrong   200 *embattailèd and ranked* ready for battle and arrayed in proper order   201 *artificer* workman, artisan   202 *Cuts off his* interrupts the tailor's   205 *cause* reason   207 *No had* had I not; *provoke* prompt   208 *attended* served   209 *humors* whims; *warrant* command   210 *within* into; *house of life* body   211 *winking of authority* failure of the king to enforce the law

To understand a law, to know the meaning   212
Of dangerous majesty, when, perchance, it frowns   213
More upon humor than advised respect.   214

HUBERT
Here is your hand and seal for what I did.   215

KING JOHN
O, when the last account 'twixt heaven and earth
Is to be made, then shall this hand and seal
Witness against us to damnation!
How oft the sight of means to do ill deeds
Makes deeds ill done! Hadst not thou been by,   220
A fellow by the hand of nature marked,   221
Quoted and signed to do a deed of shame,   222
This murder had not come into my mind;
But taking note of thy abhorred aspect,   224
Finding thee fit for bloody villainy,
Apt, liable to be employed in danger,   226
I faintly broke with thee of Arthur's death;   227
And thou, to be endearèd to a king,
Made it no conscience to destroy a prince.   229

HUBERT
My lord –   230

KING JOHN
Hadst thou but shook thy head or made a pause
When I spake darkly what I purposèd,   232
Or turned an eye of doubt upon my face,
As bid me tell my tale in express words,   234
Deep shame had struck me dumb, made me break off,   235
And those thy fears might have wrought fears in me.

---

212 *understand* infer   213 *dangerous* awesome   214 *upon humor* because of
a whim; *advised respect* carefully considered decision   215 *hand and seal* sig-
nature and royal notarization (by means of a waxen impression of the royal
signet ring)   221 *by . . . marked* marked out by his appearance   222 *Quoted
and signed* especially noted and marked out   224 *abhorred aspect* horrible
appearance   226 *liable* suitable   227 *faintly broke with* hesitatingly con-
fided in   229 *conscience* matter of conscience   232 *darkly* vaguely; *purposèd*
intended   234 *As* as if to; *in express words* clearly   235 *break off* stop

But thou didst understand me by my signs
238 And didst in signs again parley with sin;
239 Yea, without stop, didst let thy heart consent,
240 And consequently thy rude hand to act
The deed which both our tongues held vile to name.
Out of my sight, and never see me more!
243 My nobles leave me, and my state is braved,
244 Even at my gates, with ranks of foreign powers.
245 Nay, in the body of this fleshly land,
246 This kingdom, this confine of blood and breath,
247 Hostility and civil tumult reigns
Between my conscience and my cousin's death.

HUBERT
Arm you against your other enemies;
250 I'll make a peace between your soul and you.
Young Arthur is alive. This hand of mine
252 Is yet a maiden and an innocent hand,
Not painted with the crimson spots of blood.
Within this bosom never entered yet
255 The dreadful motion of a murderous thought,
256 And you have slandered nature in my form,
Which, howsoever rude exteriorly,
Is yet the cover of a fairer mind
Than to be butcher of an innocent child.

KING JOHN
260 Doth Arthur live? O, haste thee to the peers!
261 Throw this report on their incensèd rage,
262 And make them tame to their obedience.
Forgive the comment that my passion made
264 Upon thy feature, for my rage was blind,

---

238 *parley* negotiate, agree 239 *stop* hesitation 243 *braved* defied 244 *ranks* armies 245 *fleshly land* his human body (conceived of as a little world paralleling the physical universe in its composition) 246 *confine* territory bound by frontiers 247 *civil tumult* internal war 252 *maiden* bloodless 255 *motion* impulse 256 *form* outward appearance 260 *peers* nobles 261 *Throw* i.e., as water, to quench the fire of rage; *incensèd* inflamed 262 *obedience* i.e., to the king 264 *feature* appearance

And foul imaginary eyes of blood   265
Presented thee more hideous than thou art.
O, answer not, but to my closet bring   267
The angry lords with all expedient haste.
I conjure thee but slowly; run more fast.   *Exeunt.*   269

*

❧   **IV.3**   *Enter Arthur, on the walls.*

ARTHUR
    The wall is high, and yet will I leap down.
    Good ground, be pitiful and hurt me not!
    There's few or none do know me; if they did,
    This shipboy's semblance hath disguised me quite.   4
    I am afraid, and yet I'll venture it.
    If I get down, and do not break my limbs,
    I'll find a thousand shifts to get away.   7
    As good to die and go, as die and stay. *[Leaps down.]*
    O me! My uncle's spirit is in these stones!   9
    Heaven take my soul, and England keep my bones!   10
        Dies.
        Enter Pembroke, Salisbury, and Bigot.

SALISBURY
    Lords, I will meet him at Saint Edmundsbury.   11
    It is our safety, and we must embrace   12
    This gentle offer of the perilous time.

PEMBROKE
    Who brought that letter from the cardinal?

SALISBURY
    The Count Melun, a noble lord of France,

---

265 *imaginary eyes of blood* i.e., Hubert's eyes, which in John's imagination
seemed full of blood 267 *closet* inner, private chamber 269 *conjure*
solemnly urge

   IV.3 A castle wall 4 *semblance* disguise 7 *shifts* stratagems 9 *My . . .
stones* i.e., the stones are murderously hard 11 *him* i.e., the dauphin 12
safety security; *embrace* welcome

16 Whose private with me of the dauphin's love
17 Is much more general than these lines import.

BIGOT
    Tomorrow morning let us meet him then.

SALISBURY
    Or rather then set forward, for 'twill be
20 Two long days' journey, lords, or ere we meet.
        Enter Bastard.

BASTARD
21 Once more today well met, distempered lords!
22 The king by me requests your presence straight.

SALISBURY
    The king hath dispossessed himself of us.
    We will not line his thin bestainèd cloak
25 With our pure honors, nor attend the foot
    That leaves the print of blood where'er it walks.
    Return and tell him so. We know the worst.

BASTARD
    Whate'er you think, good words, I think, were best.

SALISBURY
29 Our griefs, and not our manners, reason now.

BASTARD
30 But there is little reason in your grief;
    Therefore 'twere reason you had manners now.

PEMBROKE
32 Sir, sir, impatience hath his privilege.

BASTARD
    'Tis true, to hurt his master, no man else.

SALISBURY
    This is the prison. *[Sees Arthur.]* What is he lies here?

PEMBROKE
    O death, made proud with pure and princely beauty!

---

16 *private* private communication; *love* friendship   17 *general* comprehensive   20 *or ere* before   21 *distempered* disgruntled   22 *straight* at once   25 *attend* follow   29 *griefs* grievances; *reason* talk   32 *impatience . . . privilege* anger is not subject to the usual laws of courtesy; *privilege* license

The earth had not a hole to hide this deed.

SALISBURY
Murder, as hating what himself hath done,
Doth lay it open to urge on revenge.   38

BIGOT
Or when he doomed this beauty to a grave,
Found it too precious princely for a grave.   40

SALISBURY
Sir Richard, what think you? Have you beheld,
Or have you read or heard, or could you think,
Or do you almost think, although you see,
That you do see? Could thought, without this object,   44
Form such another? This is the very top,   45
The height, the crest, or crest unto the crest,
Of murder's arms. This is the bloodiest shame,
The wildest savagery, the vilest stroke,
That ever walleyed wrath or staring rage   49
Presented to the tears of soft remorse.   50

PEMBROKE
All murders past do stand excused in this.   51
And this, so sole and so unmatchable,   52
Shall give a holiness, a purity,
To the yet unbegotten sin of times,   54
And prove a deadly bloodshed but a jest,
Exampled by this heinous spectacle.   56

BASTARD
It is a damnèd and a bloody work,
The graceless action of a heavy hand,   58
If that it be the work of any hand.

SALISBURY
If that it be the work of any hand!   60

---

38 *open* out in the open 40 *too . . . grave* (bodies of princes were entombed
above ground) 44 *That* that which; *this object* i.e., Arthur's body 45 *top*
apex 49 *walleyed* with glaring eyes; *rage* madness 50 *remorse* pity 51 *past*
former; *stand excused* held guiltless (by comparison) 52 *sole* unique 54
times future ages 56 *Exampled by* compared with 58 *graceless* unholy;
heavy wicked

61 We had a kind of light what would ensue.
It is the shameful work of Hubert's hand,
63 The practice and the purpose of the king,
From whose obedience I forbid my soul,
Kneeling before this ruin of sweet life,
And breathing to his breathless excellence
The incense of a vow, a holy vow,
Never to taste the pleasures of the world,
69 Never to be infected with delight,
70 Nor conversant with ease and idleness,
71 Till I have set a glory to this hand,
72 By giving it the worship of revenge.

PEMBROKE, BIGOT
Our souls religiously confirm thy words.
Enter Hubert.

HUBERT
Lords, I am hot with haste in seeking you.
Arthur doth live; the king hath sent for you.

SALISBURY
O, he is bold and blushes not at death.
77 Avaunt, thou hateful villain! Get thee gone!

HUBERT
78 I am no villain.

SALISBURY
[Drawing his sword]
                              Must I rob the law?

BASTARD
79 Your sword is bright, sir; put it up again.

SALISBURY
80 Not till I sheathe it in a murderer's skin.

HUBERT
Stand back, Lord Salisbury, stand back, I say!

---

61 *light* inkling **63** *practice* machination **69** *infected* diseased (delight under such circumstances is conceived of as a disease) **71** *to* upon; *this hand* i.e., his own hand raised in celebration of his vow **72** *worship* honor, dignity **77** *Avaunt* be gone **78** *rob the law* i.e., by taking justice into his own hands **79** *bright* unbloodied, clean; *up* away

By heaven, I think my sword's as sharp as yours.
I would not have you, lord, forget yourself,
Nor tempt the danger of my true defense,   84
Lest I, by marking of your rage, forget   85
Your worth, your greatness, and nobility.

BIGOT
Out, dunghill! Dar'st thou brave a nobleman?   87

HUBERT
Not for my life, but yet I dare defend
My innocent life against an emperor.

SALISBURY
Thou art a murderer.   90

HUBERT   Do not prove me so.
Yet I am none. Whose tongue soe'er speaks false,
Not truly speaks; who speaks not truly, lies.

PEMBROKE
Cut him to pieces.

BASTARD   Keep the peace, I say.

SALISBURY
Stand by, or I shall gall you, Faulconbridge.   94

BASTARD
Thou wert better gall the devil, Salisbury.
If thou but frown on me, or stir thy foot,
Or teach thy hasty spleen to do me shame,   97
I'll strike thee dead. Put up thy sword betime,   98
Or I'll so maul you and your toasting iron   99
That you shall think the devil is come from hell.   100

BIGOT
What wilt thou do, renownèd Faulconbridge?
Second a villain and a murderer?   102

HUBERT
Lord Bigot, I am none.

---

84 *tempt* risk; *true defense* (1) honest defense of my cause, (2) skillful use of
my sword   85 *marking of* (1) observing, (2) striking a blow at   87 *brave* insult   90 *Do . . . so* i.e., by compelling me to kill you   94 *by* aside; *gall* injure
97 *spleen* wrath   98 *betime* at once   99 *toasting iron* sword (a term of contempt)   102 *Second* support

BIGOT   Who killed this prince?

HUBERT
'Tis not an hour since I left him well.
I honored him, I loved him, and will weep
106   My date of life out for his sweet life's loss.

SALISBURY
Trust not those cunning waters of his eyes,
For villainy is not without such rheum,
109   And he, long traded in it, makes it seem
110   Like rivers of remorse and innocency.
Away with me, all you whose souls abhor
112   Th' uncleanly savors of a slaughterhouse,
For I am stifled with this smell of sin.

BIGOT
Away toward Bury, to the dauphin there!

PEMBROKE
115   There tell the king he may inquire us out.

                              Exeunt Lords.

BASTARD
Here's a good world! Knew you of this fair work?
Beyond the infinite and boundless reach
Of mercy, if thou didst this deed of death,
Art thou damned, Hubert.

HUBERT   Do but hear me, sir.

BASTARD
120   Ha! I'll tell thee what.
121   Thou'rt damned as black – nay, nothing is so black.
122   Thou art more deep damned than Prince Lucifer.
There is not yet so ugly a fiend of hell
As thou shalt be, if thou didst kill this child.

HUBERT
Upon my soul –

BASTARD   If thou didst but consent

---

106 *date* duration   **109** *long traded* experienced   **112** *savors* odors   **115** *inquire us out* ask or seek for us   **121** *black* (the traditional color of the devil and of all damned souls)   **122** *Prince Lucifer* i.e., the devil

To this most cruel act, do but despair,
And if thou want'st a cord, the smallest thread   127
That ever spider twisted from her womb
Will serve to strangle thee; a rush will be a beam   129
To hang thee on. Or wouldst thou drown thyself,   130
Put but a little water in a spoon,
And it shall be as all the ocean,
Enough to stifle such a villain up.   133
I do suspect thee very grievously.   134

HUBERT
If I in act, consent, or sin of thought,
Be guilty of the stealing that sweet breath
Which was embounded in this beauteous clay,   137
Let hell want pains enough to torture me.
I left him well.

BASTARD   Go, bear him in thine arms.
I am amazed, methinks, and lose my way   140
Among the thorns and dangers of this world.
How easy dost thou take all England up!   142
From forth this morsel of dead royalty   143
The life, the right and truth of all this realm
Is fled to heaven, and England now is left
To tug and scramble and to part by th' teeth
The unowed interest of proud-swelling state.   147
Now for the bare-picked bone of majesty
Doth doggèd war bristle his angry crest   149
And snarleth in the gentle eyes of peace.   150
Now powers from home and discontents at home   151
Meet in one line, and vast confusion waits,   152
As doth a raven on a sick-fallen beast,

---

127 *a cord* i.e., to hang himself with   129 *rush* slender reed   133 *stifle* smother   134 *grievously* extremely   137 *embounded . . . clay* enclosed within this beautiful body   140 *amazed* bewildered   142 *thou* Hubert; *take . . . up* lift up Arthur's body   143 *morsel* fragment, small piece   147 *unowed interest* disputed ownership   149 *doggèd* (1) fierce, (2) like a dog   151 *from home* foreign; *discontents* rebels   152 *in one line* together

154 The imminent decay of wrested pomp.
155 Now happy he whose cloak and ceinture can
Hold out this tempest. Bear away that child,
And follow me with speed. I'll to the king.
158 A thousand businesses are brief in hand,
And heaven itself doth frown upon the land. *[Exeunt.]*

*

~ **V.1** *Enter King John and Pandulph,
[with] Attendants.*

KING JOHN
Thus have I yielded up into your hand
2 The circle of my glory.
PANDULPH *[Giving King John the crown]*
Take again
3 From this my hand, as holding of the pope,
Your sovereign greatness and authority.
KING JOHN
Now keep your holy word. Go meet the French,
6 And from his holiness use all your power
To stop their marches 'fore we are inflamed.
8 Our discontented counties do revolt.
Our people quarrel with obedience,
10 Swearing allegiance and the love of soul
11 To stranger blood, to foreign royalty.
12 This inundation of mistempered humor
13 Rests by you only to be qualified.
Then pause not, for the present time's so sick,

---

154 *wrested pomp* usurped kingship 155 *ceinture* belt 158 *businesses* tasks;
brief in hand calling for immediate attention
    V.1 The English court 2 *circle* crown 3 *as holding* by the authority of
6 *his holiness* i.e., the pope 8 *counties* shires or noblemen 10 *love of soul*
deepest love, loyalty 11 *stranger* alien 12 *inundation . . . humor* overgrowth, because of disorder, of one of the four elements of the body (John is
drawing his metaphor from current medical terminology) 13 *Rests . . .
qualified* can be reduced to proper proportions only by you

That present med'cine must be ministered,   15
Or overthrow incurable ensues.   16

PANDULPH
    It was my breath that blew this tempest up,
    Upon your stubborn usage of the pope,   18
    But since you are a gentle convertite,   19
    My tongue shall hush again this storm of war   20
    And make fair weather in your blust'ring land.
    On this Ascension Day, remember well,
    Upon your oath of service to the pope,
    Go I to make the French lay down their arms.   *Exit.*

KING JOHN
    Is this Ascension Day? Did not the prophet
    Say that before Ascension Day at noon
    My crown I should give off? Even so I have.   27
    I did suppose it should be on constraint,   28
    But, heaven be thanked, it is but voluntary.
        Enter Bastard.

BASTARD
    All Kent hath yielded; nothing there holds out   30
    But Dover Castle. London hath received,
    Like a kind host, the dauphin and his powers.
    Your nobles will not hear you, but are gone
    To offer service to your enemy,
    And wild amazement hurries up and down   35
    The little number of your doubtful friends.   36

KING JOHN
    Would not my lords return to me again
    After they heard young Arthur was alive?

BASTARD
    They found him dead and cast into the streets,
    An empty casket, where the jewel of life   40

---

15 *ministered* administered   16 *overthrow* destruction   18 *Upon* because of; *usage* treatment   19 *convertite* convert   27 *give off* relinquish   28 *on constraint* by force   35 *amazement* bewilderment   36 *doubtful* (1) frightened, (2) of questionable loyalty   40 *casket* jewelry box

By some damned hand was robbed and ta'en away.

KING JOHN

    That villain Hubert told me he did live.

BASTARD

43   So, on my soul, he did, for aught he knew.
    But wherefore do you droop? Why look you sad?
    Be great in act, as you have been in thought.
    Let not the world see fear and sad distrust
    Govern the motion of a kingly eye.
48   Be stirring as the time; be fire with fire.
49   Threaten the threat'ner, and outface the brow
50   Of bragging horror. So shall inferior eyes,
    That borrow their behaviors from the great,
    Grow great by your example and put on
    The dauntless spirit of resolution.
    Away, and glisten like the god of war
55   When he intendeth to become the field.
    Show boldness and aspiring confidence.
    What, shall they seek the lion in his den
    And fright him there? And make him tremble there?
59   O, let it not be said! Forage, and run
60   To meet displeasure farther from the doors,
61   And grapple with him ere he come so nigh.

KING JOHN

    The legate of the pope hath been with me,
63   And I have made a happy peace with him,
    And he hath promised to dismiss the powers
65   Led by the dauphin.

BASTARD   O inglorious league!

66   Shall we, upon the footing of our land,
67   Send fair-play orders and make compromise,
68   Insinuation, parley, and base truce

---

43 *aught* all 48 *stirring* energetic 49 *outface* stare down 50 *inferior* lesser-born 55 *become* adorn 59 *Forage* seek out the enemy 61 *nigh* near 63 *happy* favorable 65 *league* alliance 66 *footing* i.e., trampling upon by foreign armies 67 *fair-play orders* chivalric stipulations 68 *Insinuation* self-ingratiation; *base truce* ignoble league

To arms invasive? Shall a beardless boy,   69
A cockered silken wanton, brave our fields   70
And flesh his spirit in a warlike soil,   71
Mocking the air with colors idly spread,   72
And find no check? Let us, my liege, to arms!   73
Perchance the cardinal cannot make your peace;
Or if he do, let it at least be said
They saw we had a purpose of defense.   76

KING JOHN
Have thou the ordering of this present time.   77

BASTARD
Away then, with good courage! Yet, I know,
Our party may well meet a prouder foe.   *Exeunt.*   79

*

∾ **V.2** *Enter (in arms) [Lewis the] Dauphin, Salisbury,*
Melun, Pembroke, Bigot, Soldiers.

LEWIS
My Lord Melun, let this be copied out,
And keep it safe for our remembrance.
Return the precedent to those lords again,   3
That, having our fair order written down,   4
Both they and we, perusing o'er these notes,
May know wherefore we took the Sacrament,   6
And keep our faiths firm and inviolable.

SALISBURY
Upon our sides it never shall be broken.

---

69 *arms invasive* invading armies **70** *cockered* pampered; *silken* (1) tender,
(2) clothed in fine garments; *wanton* spoilt child; *brave* (1) insult, (2) display
his finery in **71** *flesh* initiate in bloodshed; *warlike soil* martial land **72** *colors* standard, battle flag; *idly* carelessly **73** *check* resistance; *liege* lord **76**
purpose of intention to **77** *ordering* i.e., command over the organization (of
a defense); *present* immediate **79** *prouder* more powerful
   V.2 The French camp **3** *precedent* first draft of treaty **4** *fair order* equitable conditions **6** *Sacrament* (the lords took Communion in order to sanctify the treaty)

And, noble dauphin, albeit we swear
10   A voluntary zeal and an unurgèd faith
To your proceedings, yet believe me, prince,
12   I am not glad that such a sore of time
13   Should seek a plaster by contemned revolt,
14   And heal the inveterate canker of one wound
By making many. O, it grieves my soul
16   That I must draw this metal from my side
To be a widow maker! O, and there
Where honorable rescue and defense
19   Cries out upon the name of Salisbury.
20   But such is the infection of the time
21   That, for the health and physic of our right,
22   We cannot deal but with the very hand
Of stern injustice and confusèd wrong.
24   And is 't not pity, O my grievèd friends,
That we, the sons and children of this isle,
Were born to see so sad an hour as this,
Wherein we step after a stranger, march
28   Upon her gentle bosom, and fill up
29   Her enemies' ranks – I must withdraw and weep
30   Upon the spot of this enforcèd cause –
31   To grace the gentry of a land remote,
32   And follow unacquainted colors here?
33   What, here? O nation, that thou couldst remove!
34   That Neptune's arms, who clippeth thee about,
35   Would bear thee from the knowledge of thyself,
36   And grapple thee unto a pagan shore,

---

10 *unurgèd* uncompelled   **12** *sore of time* present injury, distress   **13** *plaster* dressing for a wound; *contemned* despised   **14** *inveterate canker* chronic sore   **16** *metal* sword   **19** *Cries out upon* appeals to   **21** *physic of* remedy for   **22** *deal* act   **24** *grievèd* unhappy   **28** *her* i.e., England's   **29** *ranks* armies   **30** *spot* disgrace; *enforcèd* forced upon us   **31** *grace* pay homage to   **32** *unacquainted colors* foreign banners   **33** *remove* move yourself, depart   **34** *clippeth* embraces   **35** *bear* carry away; *knowledge* awareness   **36** *grapple* attach, bind (e.g., with grappling hooks); *pagan* foreign, non-Christian

Where these two Christian armies might combine   37
The blood of malice in a vein of league,   38
And not to spend it so unneighborly!
LEWIS
A noble temper dost thou show in this,   40
And great affections wrestling in thy bosom   41
Doth make an earthquake of nobility.
O, what a noble combat hast thou fought
Between compulsion and a brave respect!   44
Let me wipe off this honorable dew,   45
That silverly doth progress on thy cheeks.   46
My heart hath melted at a lady's tears,
Being an ordinary inundation,   48
But this effusion of such manly drops,
This shower, blown up by tempest of the soul,   50
Startles mine eyes, and makes me more amazed
Than had I seen the vaulty top of heaven   52
Figured quite o'er with burning meteors.   53
Lift up thy brow, renownèd Salisbury,
And with a great heart heave away this storm.
Commend these waters to those baby eyes   56
That never saw the giant world enraged,
Nor met with fortune other than at feasts,
Full warm of blood, of mirth, of gossiping.   59
Come, come; for thou shalt thrust thy hand as deep   60
Into the purse of rich prosperity
As Lewis himself. So, nobles, shall you all,
That knit your sinews to the strength of mine.
     Enter Pandulph.

----

37 *combine* join   38 *vein* (1) blood vessel, (2) mood   40 *temper* state of
mind   41 *affections* emotions   44 *compulsion* what you were forced to do;
brave respect courageous consideration of your true duty   45 *dew* i.e., tears
46 *progress* move slowly (like a king or queen in state; the metaphor empha-
sizes the nobility of Salisbury's tears)   48 *ordinary inundation* frequent, or
usual, downpour   52 *vaulty* vaulted (as a cathedral roof)   53 *Figured* deco-
rated   56 *Commend* leave   59 *Full . . . blood* full of human feeling

64 And even there, methinks, an angel spake.
65 Look, where the holy legate comes apace,
66 To give us warrant from the hand of heaven,
67 And on our actions set the name of right
   With holy breath.

PANDULPH   Hail, noble prince of France!

69 The next is this: King John hath reconciled
70 Himself to Rome; his spirit is come in
   That so stood out against the holy church,
72 The great metropolis and see of Rome.
73 Therefore thy threat'ning colors now wind up,
   And tame the savage spirit of wild war,
75 That, like a lion fostered up at hand,
   It may lie gently at the foot of peace,
77 And be no further harmful than in show.

LEWIS

78 Your grace shall pardon me; I will not back.
79 I am too highborn to be propertied,
80 To be a secondary at control,
   Or useful servingman and instrument
   To any sovereign state throughout the world.
   Your breath first kindled the dead coal of wars
   Between this chastised kingdom and myself,
85 And brought in matter that should feed this fire;
   And now 'tis far too huge to be blown out
   With that same weak wind which enkindled it.
   You taught me how to know the face of right,
89 Acquainted me with interest to this land,

---

64 *an angel spake* (1) Pandulph, the angel since he bears heaven's warrant, has just entered, (2) a pun on "angel," a coin, with contemptuous reference to the dauphin's mercenary motives   **65** *apace* hurriedly   **66** *warrant* authorization   **67** *set* i.e., like a seal upon a warrant   **69** *next* news, latest event   **70** *is come in* has submitted   **72** *see* jurisdiction   **73** *wind up* furl   **75** *fostered* raised   **77** *in show* in appearance only   **78** *shall* must; *back* retreat   **79** *propertied* treated like property, made a tool of   **80** *secondary at control* agent controlled by another   **85** *matter* fuel   **89** *interest to* claim in

Yea, thrust this enterprise into my heart;   90
And come ye now to tell me John hath made
His peace with Rome? What is that peace to me?
I, by the honor of my marriage bed,
After young Arthur, claim this land for mine,
And, now it is half-conquered, must I back
Because that John hath made his peace with Rome?
Am I Rome's slave? What penny hath Rome borne,   97
What men provided, what munition sent,
To underprop this action? Is 't not I   99
That undergo this charge? Who else but I,   100
And such as to my claim are liable,   101
Sweat in this business and maintain this war?
Have I not heard these islanders shout out,   103
Vive le roi! as I have banked their towns?   104
Have I not here the best cards for the game
To win this easy match played for a crown?
And shall I now give o'er the yielded set?   107
No, no, on my soul, it never shall be said.

PANDULPH
You look but on the outside of this work.   109

LEWIS
Outside or inside, I will not return   110
Till my attempt so much be glorified
As to my ample hope was promisèd   112
Before I drew this gallant head of war,   113
And culled these fiery spirits from the world,   114
To outlook conquest and to win renown   115
Even in the jaws of danger and of death.
     [Trumpet sounds.]

---

97 _borne_ spent   99 _underprop_ support   100 _charge_ expense   101 _liable_ subject   103 _these islanders_ i.e., English citizens   104 _Vive le roi_ Long live the king (French); _banked_ sailed by   107 _give o'er_ abandon; _yielded set_ game already forfeited to me   109 _outside_ external appearance, immediate gains (as opposed to more devious political consequences)   112 _ample hope_ great expectation   113 _head_ army   114 _culled_ carefully selected   115 _outlook_ stare down

117 What lusty trumpet thus doth summon us?
       Enter Bastard.

BASTARD

118 According to the fair play of the world,
119 Let me have audience; I am sent to speak.
120 My holy Lord of Milan, from the king
121 I come, to learn how you have dealt for him,
122 And, as you answer, I do know the scope
123 And warrant limited unto my tongue.

PANDULPH

124 The dauphin is too willful-opposite,
125 And will not temporize with my entreaties.
126 He flatly says he'll not lay down his arms.

BASTARD

       By all the blood that ever fury breathed,
       The youth says well. Now hear our English king,
129 For thus his royalty doth speak in me.
130 He is prepared, and reason too he should.
131 This apish and unmannerly approach,
132 This harnessed masque and unadvisèd revel,
       This unheard sauciness and boyish troops,
       The king doth smile at, and is well prepared
       To whip this dwarfish war, these pygmy arms,
136 From out the circle of his territories.
137 That hand which had the strength, even at your door,
138 To cudgel you and make you take the hatch,
       To dive, like buckets, in concealèd wells,
140 To crouch in litter of your stable planks,

---

117 *lusty* vigorous 118 *fair play* rules of chivalry 119 *have audience* be heard; *to speak* i.e., rather than to fight 121 *for him* on his behalf, by him 122 *as* according as; *scope* latitude 123 *limited* appointed 124 *willful-opposite* stubbornly hostile 125 *temporize* come to terms 126 *flatly* bluntly, outright 129 *royalty . . . me* I present his royal will 130 *prepared* i.e., to fight; *reason too* justifiably so 131 *apish* fantastic 132 *harnessed* in armor; *masque* theatrical entertainment; *unadvisèd revel* thoughtless entertainment 136 *circle* compass 137 *door* doorstep (i.e., Calais) 138 *take the hatch* leap over a half door or stile (like beaten dogs fleeing their masters) 140 *litter* bedding (for animals); *planks* floors

To lie like pawns locked up in chests and trunks,   141
To hug with swine, to seek sweet safety out   142
In vaults and prisons, and to thrill and shake
Even at the crying of your nation's crow,   144
Thinking this voice an armèd Englishman –
Shall that victorious hand be feebled here   146
That in your chambers gave you chastisement?
No! Know the gallant monarch is in arms,
And like an eagle o'er his aerie towers,   149
To souse annoyance that comes near his nest.   150
And you degenerate, you ingrate revolts,   151
You bloody Neroes, ripping up the womb   152
Of your dear mother England, blush for shame;
For your own ladies and pale-visaged maids   154
Like Amazons come tripping after drums,   155
Their thimbles into armèd gauntlets change,   156
Their needles to lances, and their gentle hearts   157
To fierce and bloody inclination.   158

LEWIS
There end thy brave, and turn thy face in peace.   159
We grant thou canst outscold us. Fare thee well.   160
We hold our time too precious to be spent
With such a brabbler.   162

PANDULPH   Give me leave to speak.

BASTARD
No, I will speak.   163

LEWIS   We will attend to neither.

---

141 *pawns* articles in pawn   142 *hug with* embrace, cosy up to   144 *your nation's crow* sound of the rooster, traditional symbol of France   146 *feebled* enfeebled, weak   149 *aerie* eagle's nest; *towers* soars   150 *souse* swoop down on (like a bird of prey); *annoyance* threat of danger   151 *ingrate revolts* ungrateful rebels   152 *Neroes* (the Roman emperor Nero was said to have ripped open his mother's womb after murdering her)   154 *pale-visaged* white-skinned   155 *Amazons* female warriors of Greek mythology   156 *gauntlets* gloves   157 *needles* (monosyllable; in folio, "Needl's")   158 *inclination* (1) disposition, (2) the slanting position of a knight charging with a lance (a quibble)   159 *brave* defiant boast   160 *grant* concede that   162 *brabbler* braggart   163 *attend* listen

Strike up the drums, and let the tongue of war
Plead for our interest and our being here.

BASTARD

Indeed, your drums, being beaten, will cry out,
And so shall you, being beaten. Do but start
An echo with the clamor of thy drum,
169 And even at hand a drum is ready braced
170 That shall reverberate all as loud as thine.
Sound but another, and another shall
172 As loud as thine rattle the welkin's ear
And mock the deep-mouthed thunder. For at hand –
174 Not trusting to this halting legate here,
Whom he hath used rather for sport than need –
Is warlike John; and in his forehead sits
177 A bare-ribbed death, whose office is this day
To feast upon whole thousands of the French.

LEWIS

Strike up our drums to find this danger out.

BASTARD

180 And thou shalt find it, dauphin, do not doubt.

Exeunt.

*

◆ **V.3** *Alarums. Enter [King] John and Hubert.*

KING JOHN

How goes the day with us? O, tell me, Hubert.

HUBERT

Badly, I fear. How fares your majesty?

KING JOHN

This fever that hath troubled me so long
Lies heavy on me. O, my heart is sick!

---

169 *ready* at the ready, prepared; *braced* with tightened skin, ready for playing   **172** *welkin's* sky's   **174** *halting* wavering, ineffectual   **177** *bare-ribbed death* i.e., death conceived of as a skeleton; *office* function
V.3 The English camp

Enter a Messenger.

MESSENGER
My lord, your valiant kinsman, Faulconbridge,
Desires your majesty to leave the field   6
And send him word by me which way you go.

KING JOHN
Tell him, toward Swinstead, to the abbey there.   8

MESSENGER
Be of good comfort, for the great supply   9
That was expected by the dauphin here,   10
Are wracked three nights ago on Goodwin sands.   11
This news was brought to Richard but even now.
The French fight coldly and retire themselves.   13

KING JOHN
Ay me! This tyrant fever burns me up,   14
And will not let me welcome this good news.
Set on toward Swinstead. To my litter straight;   16
Weakness possesseth me, and I am faint.   *Exeunt.*

✳

☙ **V.4** *Enter Salisbury, Pembroke, and Bigot.*

SALISBURY
I did not think the king so stored with friends.   1

PEMBROKE
Up once again; put spirit in the French.
If they miscarry we miscarry too.

SALISBURY
That misbegotten devil, Faulconbridge,
In spite of spite, alone upholds the day.   5

---

6 *leave the field* retire from the battlefield   8 *Swinstead* town in Yorkshire (an
error for "Swineshead")   9 *supply* reinforcements   11 *wracked* shipwrecked;
Goodwin sands shoal off the coast of Kent   13 *coldly* without enthusiasm; *re-*
tire themselves retreat   14 *tyrant* merciless   16 *litter* traveling bed; *straight*
immediately
   V.4 The French camp   1 *stored* provided   5 *In spite of spite* despite anything we can do

PEMBROKE
> They say King John, sore sick, hath left the field.
>   *Enter Melun wounded.*

MELUN
7   Lead me to the revolts of England here.

SALISBURY
> When we were happy we had other names.

PEMBROKE
> It is the Count Melun.

SALISBURY   Wounded to death.

MELUN
10   Fly, noble English; you are bought and sold.
11   Unthread the rude eye of rebellion,
12   And welcome home again discarded faith.
>   Seek out King John and fall before his feet,
14   For if the French be lords of this loud day,
15   He means to recompense the pains you take
>   By cutting off your heads. Thus hath he sworn,
>   And I with him, and many more with me,
>   Upon the altar at Saint Edmundsbury,
>   Even on that altar where we swore to you
20   Dear amity and everlasting love.

SALISBURY
> May this be possible? May this be true?

MELUN
> Have I not hideous death within my view,
23   Retaining but a quantity of life,
24   Which bleeds away, even as a form of wax
25   Resolveth from his figure 'gainst the fire?
>   What in the world should make me now deceive,

---

7 *revolts* rebels   10 *bought and sold* betrayed   11 *Unthread ... eye* retrace
your steps (as a thread is withdrawn from the needle's eye)   12 *faith* loyalty
14 *loud* noisy   15 *He* i.e., the dauphin; *recompense the pains* reward your efforts   23 *quantity* small amount   24–25 *as a form ... fire* (witches were said
to destroy their enemies by melting waxen images of them before a fire)   25
Resolveth dissolves; *his figure* its shape

Since I must lose the use of all deceit?   27
Why should I then be false, since it is true
That I must die here and live hence by truth?   29
I say again, if Lewis do win the day,   30
He is forsworn if e'er those eyes of yours   31
Behold another day break in the east.
But even this night, whose black contagious breath   33
Already smokes about the burning crest   34
Of the old, feeble, and day-wearied sun,
Even this ill night, your breathing shall expire,   36
Paying the fine of rated treachery   37
Even with a treacherous fine of all your lives,   38
If Lewis by your assistance win the day.
Commend me to one Hubert with your king.   40
The love of him, and this respect besides,   41
For that my grandsire was an Englishman,   42
Awakes my conscience to confess all this.
In lieu whereof, I pray you, bear me hence   44
From forth the noise and rumor of the field,   45
Where I may think the remnant of my thoughts
In peace, and part this body and my soul
With contemplation and devout desires.

SALISBURY

We do believe thee, and beshrew my soul   49
But I do love the favor and the form   50
Of this most fair occasion, by the which
We will untread the steps of damnèd flight,   52
And like a bated and retirèd flood,   53

---

27 *use* profit, advantage   **29** *live hence by truth* i.e., he will live in heaven to
the extent that he has been truthful on earth   **31** *forsworn* perjured   **33** *contagious* bearing disease   **34** *smokes* grows misty (as evening approaches)   **36**
breathing breath, life   **37** *fine* penalty; *rated* (1) exposed at its true value, (2)
rebuked, punished   **38** *fine* end (with pun on "financial penalty")   **41** *respect* consideration   **42** *For that* because   **44** *In lieu whereof* in payment for
which   **45** *rumor* noise   **49** *beshrew* a curse upon   **50** *favor and the form*
outward appearance   **52** *untread* retrace   **53** *bated* abated

54   Leaving our rankness and irregular course,
55   Stoop low within those bounds we have o'erlooked,
      And calmly run on in obedience
      Even to our ocean, to our great King John.
      My arm shall give thee help to bear thee hence,
      For I do see the cruel pangs of death
60   Right in thine eye. Away, my friends! New flight,
61   And happy newness, that intends old right.

                              Exeunt [leading off Melun].

                              *

∞ **V.5** *Enter [Lewis the] Dauphin, and his train.*

LEWIS

1   The sun of heaven methought was loath to set,
2   But stayed and made the western welkin blush,
3   When English measured backward their own ground
4   In faint retire. O, bravely came we off,
5   When with a volley of our needless shot,
      After such bloody toil, we bid good night
7   And wound our tott'ring colors clearly up,
      Last in the field, and almost lords of it!
      Enter a Messenger.

MESSENGER
      Where is my prince, the dauphin?
LEWIS   Here. What news?
MESSENGER
10   The Count Melun is slain. The English lords,
11   By his persuasion, are again fall'n off,

---

54 *rankness* overgrowth   **55** *bounds* banks, boundaries; *o'erlooked* overflowed
60 *Right* clearly   **61** *happy newness* propitious change
    V.5 The French camp   **1** *loath* reluctant   **2** *welkin* sky   **3** *measured backward* marked off with retreating steps   **4** *faint retire* timid retreat; *bravely* excellently; *came we off* we retired from battle   **5** *needless* (1) unnecessary, (2) superfluous   **7** *tott'ring* (1) wavering, (2) in tatters (rags); *colors* banners; *clearly* neatly, without interference from the enemy   **11** *are again fall'n off* have again broken faith

And your supply, which you have wished so long, 12
Are cast away and sunk on Goodwin sands.

LEWIS
Ah, foul, shrewd news! Beshrew thy very heart! 14
I did not think to be so sad tonight
As this hath made me. Who was he that said
King John did fly an hour or two before 17
The stumbling night did part our weary powers? 18

MESSENGER
Whoever spoke it, it is true, my lord.

LEWIS
Well, keep good quarter and good care tonight. 20
The day shall not be up so soon as I
To try the fair adventure of tomorrow. *Exeunt.* 22

*

❧ **V.6** *Enter Bastard and Hubert, severally.*

HUBERT
Who's there? Speak, ho! Speak quickly, or I shoot.

BASTARD
A friend. What art thou? 2

HUBERT   Of the part of England.

BASTARD
Whither dost thou go?

HUBERT
What's that to thee? Why may not I demand 4
Of thine affairs as well as thou of mine?

BASTARD
Hubert, I think? 6

HUBERT   Thou hast a perfect thought.

---

12 *supply* reinforcements   14 *shrewd* grievous, bitter; *Beshrew* curse   17 *fly* flee   18 *stumbling* causing to stumble   20 *quarter* watch   22 *fair adventure* good fortune
  V.6 The English camp   2 *Of the part* on the side   4–5 *demand . . . affairs* ask you about your business   6 *perfect* correct

7   I will upon all hazards well believe
Thou art my friend, that know'st my tongue so well.
Who art thou?

BASTARD   Who thou wilt; and if thou please,

10   Thou mayst befriend me so much as to think

11   I come one way of the Plantagenets.

HUBERT

12   Unkind remembrance! Thou and eyeless night

13   Have done me shame. Brave soldier, pardon me,

14   That any accent breaking from thy tongue

15   Should scape the true acquaintance of mine ear.

BASTARD

16   Come, come! Sans compliment, what news abroad?

HUBERT

17   Why, here walk I in the black brow of night
To find you out.

BASTARD   Brief, then; and what's the news?

HUBERT

O, my sweet sir, news fitting to the night,

20   Black, fearful, comfortless, and horrible.

BASTARD

Show me the very wound of this ill news.
I am no woman; I'll not swoon at it.

HUBERT

The king, I fear, is poisoned by a monk.

24   I left him almost speechless and broke out
To acquaint you with this evil, that you might

26   The better arm you to the sudden time

27   Than if you had at leisure known of this.

---

7 *upon all hazards* take a chance   11 *come one way* i.e., descend on one side
12 *remembrance* memory; *eyeless* i.e., black   13 *done me shame* disgraced me
(by causing my discourteous failure to recognize a friend)   14 *accent* speech
15 *scape* escape   16 *Sans compliment* without formal speech   17 *black brow*
dark forehead   24 *broke out* rushed away   26 *arm . . . time* prepare yourself
for the emergency; *sudden time* i.e., events that occur without warning   27
at leisure after delay

BASTARD

  How did he take it? Who did taste to him?   28

HUBERT

  A monk, I tell you, a resolvèd villain,   29

  Whose bowels suddenly burst out. The king   *30*

  Yet speaks and peradventure may recover.   31

BASTARD

  Whom didst thou leave to tend his majesty?

HUBERT

  Why, know you not? The lords are all come back,

  And brought Prince Henry in their company,

  At whose request the king hath pardoned them,

  And they are all about his majesty.

BASTARD

  Withhold thine indignation, mighty heaven,

  And tempt us not to bear above our power!   38

  I'll tell thee, Hubert, half my power this night,   39

  Passing these flats, are taken by the tide.   40

  These Lincoln Washes have devourèd them.   41

  Myself, well mounted, hardly have escaped.   42

  Away before! Conduct me to the king;

  I doubt he will be dead or ere I come.   *Exeunt.* 44

*

∾ **V.7** *Enter Prince Henry, Salisbury, and Bigot.*

PRINCE HENRY

  It is too late. The life of all his blood

  Is touched corruptibly, and his pure brain,   2

  Which some suppose the soul's frail dwelling house,

---

28 *taste to* serve as food taster for **29** *resolvèd* determined **31** *Yet* still; *per-adventure* perhaps **38** *tempt . . . power* do not test us by making us endure more than we are able to **39** *power* army **40** *flats* low lands near the sea **41** *Lincoln Washes* bay near Lincoln with many sandbanks **42** *well mounted* well horsed; *hardly* barely **44** *doubt* fear

    V.7 The English court **2** *touched corruptibly* infected so as to cause corruption

4   Doth, by the idle comments that it makes,

5   Foretell the ending of mortality.

     Enter Pembroke.

PEMBROKE

    His highness yet doth speak, and holds belief

    That, being brought into the open air,

    It would allay the burning quality

9   Of that fell poison which assaileth him.

PRINCE HENRY

10   Let him be brought into the orchard here.

11   Doth he still rage?   *[Exit Bigot.]*

PEMBROKE   He is more patient

    Than when you left him; even now he sung.

PRINCE HENRY

13   O, vanity of sickness! Fierce extremes

14   In their continuance will not feel themselves.

    Death, having preyed upon the outward parts,

16   Leaves them invisible, and his siege is now

    Against the mind, the which he pricks and wounds

18   With many legions of strange fantasies,

19   Which, in their throng and press to that last hold,

20   Confound themselves. 'Tis strange that death should sing.

21   I am the cygnet to this pale faint swan,

    Who chants a doleful hymn to his own death,

    And from the organ pipe of frailty sings

    His soul and body to their lasting rest.

SALISBURY

    Be of good comfort, prince, for you are born

---

4 *idle* foolish, delirious 5 *mortality* life 9 *fell* cruel 11 *rage* rave 13 *extremes* extremities 14 *In . . . themselves* as they continue, cease to be felt 16 *invisible* invisibly (modifies *Death*) 18 *legions* armies, multitudes; *fantasies* hallucinations 19 *throng and press* disordered rush; *hold* stronghold (the mind) 20 *Confound themselves* destroy one another (i.e., his delirious thoughts negate one another so that he is totally incoherent) 21 *cygnet* young swan (the swan was said to sing only one song during its life, just before its death)

To set a form upon that indigest   26
Which he hath left so shapeless and so rude.
    [King] John brought in.

KING JOHN
Ay, marry, now my soul hath elbowroom.
It would not out at windows, nor at doors.   29
There is so hot a summer in my bosom   30
That all my bowels crumble up to dust.   31
I am a scribbled form, drawn with a pen   32
Upon a parchment, and against this fire
Do I shrink up.

PRINCE HENRY   How fares your majesty?

KING JOHN
Poisoned – ill fare! Dead, forsook, cast off,   35
And none of you will bid the winter come
To thrust his icy fingers in my maw,   37
Nor let my kingdom's rivers take their course
Through my burned bosom, nor entreat the north   39
To make his bleak winds kiss my parchèd lips   40
And comfort me with cold. I do not ask you much.
I beg cold comfort; and you are so strait   42
And so ingrateful, you deny me that.

PRINCE HENRY
O, that there were some virtue in my tears   44
That might relieve you.

KING JOHN   The salt in them is hot.
Within me is a hell, and there the poison
Is as a fiend confined to tyrannize   47
On unreprievable condemnèd blood.   48
    Enter Bastard.

BASTARD
O, I am scalded with my violent motion   49

---

26 *indigest* shapeless mass, state of confusion **29** *out* escape, depart **30** *bosom* interior **31** *bowels* internal organs **32** *scribbled form* scrawled figure **35** *ill fare* (1) ill lot, (2) bad food **37** *maw* throat **39** *north* north wind **42** *strait* stingy **44** *virtue* healing power **47** *fiend* devil; *confined* imprisoned **48** *unreprievable* beyond reprieve **49** *scalded* heated

50   And spleen of speed to see your majesty.

KING JOHN

51   O cousin, thou art come to set mine eye!
52   The tackle of my heart is cracked and burnt,
53   And all the shrouds wherewith my life should sail
      Are turnèd to one thread, one little hair.
55   My heart hath one poor string to stay it by,
      Which holds but till thy news be utterèd,
57   And then all this thou seest is but a clod
58   And module of confounded royalty.

BASTARD

59   The dauphin is preparing hitherward,
60   Where God he knows how we shall answer him,
      For in a night the best part of my power,
62   As I upon advantage did remove,
63   Were in the Washes all unwarily
64   Devourèd by the unexpected flood.
          [The King dies.]

SALISBURY

65   You breathe these dead news in as dead an ear.
66   My liege! My lord! But now a king, now thus!

PRINCE HENRY

67   Even so must I run on, and even so stop.
68   What surety of the world, what hope, what stay,
      When this was now a king, and now is clay?

BASTARD

70   Art thou gone so? I do but stay behind
      To do the office for thee of revenge,

---

50 *spleen* eagerness   **51** *set mine eye* i.e., close my eyes in death   **52** *tackle* rigging of a ship   **53** *shrouds* ropes supporting the mast of a ship   **55** *stay* support   **57** *clod* lump   **58** *module* mere image; *confounded* destroyed   **59** *preparing hitherward* readying his approach, attack   **60** *answer* meet, match   **62** *upon advantage* to take advantage of a favorable opportunity; *remove* change position   **63** *unwarily* unexpectedly   **64** *unexpected flood* sudden flowing in of the tide   **65** *dead news* (1) deadly news, (2) out-of-date news   **66** *But* even; *thus* i.e., dead   **67** *run on* live out my term   **68** *surety* certainty; *stay* support   **70** *stay* remain

And then my soul shall wait on thee to heaven,   72
As it on earth hath been thy servant still.   73
Now, now, you stars that move in your right spheres,   74
Where be your powers? Show now your mended faiths,   75
And instantly return with me again,
To push destruction and perpetual shame
Out of the weak door of our fainting land.
Straight let us seek, or straight we shall be sought.   79
The dauphin rages at our very heels.   80

SALISBURY
It seems you know not, then, so much as we.
The Cardinal Pandulph is within at rest,
Who half an hour since came from the dauphin,
And brings from him such offers of our peace
As we with honor and respect may take,   85
With purpose presently to leave this war.   86

BASTARD
He will the rather do it when he sees
Ourselves well sinewèd to our defense.   88

SALISBURY
Nay, 'tis in a manner done already;
For many carriages he hath dispatched   90
To the seaside, and put his cause and quarrel
To the disposing of the cardinal;   92
With whom yourself, myself, and other lords,
If you think meet, this afternoon will post   94
To consummate this business happily.

BASTARD
Let it be so. And you, my noble prince,
With other princes that may best be spared,   97

---

72 *to* (1) in, (2) on the way to   73 *still* always   74 *stars . . . spheres* i.e., noblemen who have returned to their proper allegiance (revolving around the
throne, as stars were believed in a harmonious cosmos to revolve around the
earth)   75 *powers* armies; *mended faiths* restored loyalties   79 *Straight* immediately   85 *respect* self-respect   86 *purpose* intention; *presently* immediately   88 *sinewèd* strengthened   90 *carriages* vehicles   92 *disposing*
arbitration   94 *meet* appropriate; *post* ride   97 *princes* nobles

98   Shall wait upon your father's funeral.

PRINCE HENRY

At Worcester must his body be interred,

100   For so he willed it.

BASTARD   Thither shall it then.

101   And happily may your sweet self put on

102   The lineal state and glory of the land!

To whom, with all submission, on my knee,

104   I do bequeath my faithful services

And true subjection everlastingly. *[He kneels.]*

SALISBURY

106   And the like tender of our love we make,

107   To rest without a spot for evermore. *[The Lords kneel.]*

PRINCE HENRY

I have a kind soul that would give you thanks,

And knows not how to do it but with tears.

BASTARD   *[Rising]*

110   O, let us pay the time but needful woe,

Since it hath been beforehand with our griefs.

This England never did, nor never shall,

Lie at the proud foot of a conqueror

114   But when it first did help to wound itself.

115   Now these her princes are come home again,

116   Come the three corners of the world in arms,

117   And we shall shock them. Nought shall make us rue

If England to itself do rest but true.   *Exeunt.*

---

98 *wait upon* attend   **101** *happily* propitiously   **102** *lineal state* kingship by right of birth   **104** *bequeath* deliver, bestow   **106** *like tender* same offer   **107** *spot* blemish (of disloyalty)   **110–11** *let . . . griefs* i.e., let us not weep more than necessary, since we have already paid the sad occasion enough of the grief due to it   **114** *But* except for   **115** *Now* now that   **116** *Come* i.e., bring on, let come; *three corners* i.e., the rest of the world, England being the fourth corner   **117** *shock* meet them with force; *Nought* nothing

The distinguished Pelican Shakespeare series, newly revised
to be the premier choice for students, professors, and
general readers well into the 21st century

FOR THE BEST IN PAPERBACKS, LOOK FOR THE

In every corner of the world, on every subject under the sun, Penguin represents quality and variety—the very best in publishing today.

For complete information about books available from Penguin—including Penguin Classics, Penguin Compass, and Puffins—and how to order them, write to us at the appropriate address below. Please note that for copyright reasons the selection of books varies from country to country.

In the United States: Please write to *Penguin Group (USA), P.O. Box 12289 Dept. B, Newark, New Jersey 07101-5289* or call 1-800-788-6262.

In the United Kingdom: Please write to *Dept. EP, Penguin Books Ltd, Bath Road, Harmondsworth, West Drayton, Middlesex UB7 0DA.*

In Canada: Please write to *Penguin Books Canada Ltd, 90 Eglinton Avenue East, Suite 700, Toronto, Ontario M4P 2Y3.*

In Australia: Please write to *Penguin Books Australia Ltd, P.O. Box 257, Ringwood, Victoria 3134.*

In New Zealand: Please write to *Penguin Books (NZ) Ltd, Private Bag 102902, North Shore Mail Centre, Auckland 10.*

In India: Please write to *Penguin Books India Pvt Ltd, 11 Panchsheel Shopping Centre, Panchsheel Park, New Delhi 110 017.*

In the Netherlands: Please write to *Penguin Books Netherlands bv, Postbus 3507, NL-1001 AH Amsterdam.*

In Germany: Please write to *Penguin Books Deutschland GmbH, Metzlerstrasse 26, 60594 Frankfurt am Main.*

In Spain: Please write to *Penguin Books S. A., Bravo Murillo 19, 1° B, 28015 Madrid.*

In Italy: Please write to *Penguin Italia s.r.l., Via Benedetto Croce 2, 20094 Corsico, Milano.*

In France: Please write to *Penguin France, Le Carré Wilson, 62 rue Benjamin Baillaud, 31500 Toulouse.*

In Japan: Please write to *Penguin Books Japan Ltd, Kaneko Building, 2-3-25 Koraku, Bunkyo-Ku, Tokyo 112.*

In South Africa: Please write to *Penguin Books South Africa (Pty) Ltd, Private Bag X14, Parkview, 2122 Johannesburg.*